The Sperm Donor's Daughter
& Other Tales of Modern Family

by

Kathryn Trueblood

THE PERMANENT PRESS
SAG HARBOR, NY 11963

The stories in this collection have appeared in the following publications:
Cimarron Review, "Riptide"
Jeopardy, "In Refrain"
The Before Columbus Review, "Moonstone"

Library of Congress Cataloging-in-Publication Data

Trueblood, Kathryn.
    The Sperm Donor's Daughter & other tales of modern
        family/by Kathryn Trueblood.
      p. cm.
    ISBN   1-57962-006-X
    1. United States—Social life and customs—20th century—ficiton.
    2. Family—United States—Fiction. I. Title. II Title: Sperm
    Donor's Daughter and other tales of modern family.
    PS3570.R767S66 1998
    813'.54--DC21   97-21534
                                       CIP

THE PERMANENT PRESS
4170 Noyac Road
Sag Harbor, NY 11963

For my original mentors,
and the whole B.C.F. gang,
my literary home away from home.

Acknowledgements

Heartfelt thanks to my grandmother, my mother, and my father, each of whom encouraged my life choices in indispensable ways; and to my husband for his grace under pressure. Earnest appreciation to the readers of early drafts who saw me through, Margi Fox, Scott Driscoll, and Noel Parmentel; and to friends Laura Kalpakian, Meredith Cary, and Mary Byrne for much needed humor. Special thanks to Mary Alice Kier for her long term belief in this book and help with research. And finally gratitude to Martin and Judith Shepard who gave me the chance.

Contents

In the great quietness of these winter evenings there is one clock: the sea. Its dim momentum in the mind is the fugue upon which this writing is made.

Lawrence Durrell
Justine

The Sperm Donor's Daughter

I.

Yesterday Jessica left. This morning the tide is low and the neighborhood smells of minerals. I walk to where the road dead-ends onto mounds of oyster shells high as roof tops, piles of calcified petals clicking in the wind. Far out on the mud flats, the men from the Rock Point Company are forking oysters into wire baskets, walking slowly between the whittled marker staves. It is so quiet I can hear them sinking into the mud then breaking the suction at their heels. I smell the cranberry bogs—peat, rot, citrus and rain.

At a time when I thought my daughter's beginnings would matter least to her, I've found out the past matters most. What did I think? That she'd thank me for giving her no father? That she'd accept my record of disappointments as her own? I really don't want vindication on that score. But she's testing me. An especially truculent toddler, she would yell "One more last time." And I used to say, "This is the last last time."

It's true, she has some things to be mad about. I lied to her. I didn't tell her who her father was. Donor I.D. Number 228? I couldn't very well tell her that. His blood type perhaps? Darling, you came from the sea? And human blood is so like sea water—sodium, calcium, potassium. Who doesn't long for the Great Origin? She yearns for yearning itself; she's that age.

I gave her a love story to grow up on. Better yet I gave her a love story that would stay a love story because Carson died young and had me to miss him. Dearly beloved, dead on an airfield at Danang in '65. The shine gone out of the brown eyes beneath pale hair. How long did it take to find him? On the West Coast, we're fifteen hours behind

9

Vietnam. And I'd gone on living those days as though he were living too. Later, by telling Jess that Carson was her father, I kept him with me.

My version seemed more humane at the time, a story, not a donor insemination form. Death, birth, it seemed so random at the time. Why not tell her Carson was her father? There were plenty of fatherless babies this side of the war. But it's the deus ex machina of novels ... the Lost Dauphin, Little Lord Fauntleroy, King Arthur, Jesus even. She believes that by uncovering her heritage suddenly a true self will be revealed: nobility, power, fate. It's a fantasy route, I told her, class and position were once pretty rigidly set . She persisted.

I still want to know who I am. I asked her: what of potato peelers who give birth to geniuses? *I want to know who I am.* Perhaps she'll come back with an answer for me too, like Moses gone up the Mount. I'll finally know how to live.

I got tired of myself as subject long ago. Having Jess taught me that all those years of therapy and ascribing who-I-was-to-what-happened-when could be excised in a moment. She behaves the way she does because that's who she is: insecurities and excitements in place from Day One. I had to toss most of my carefully worked out theories that gave my parents their drubbing due. I'm sure she's working out these theories re: me right now. Maybe her father can shoulder some of this blame. Step forward, my man, we'll pin the bull's-eye right on you.

I walk the railroad tracks in my creosote-coated sneakers, passing between sand dunes and back out onto the windswept expanses. I trace my lineage through the women in my family, with my feet. I thought it would be enough, giving this to her. My grandmother once walked here; she chopped and stacked wood to resupply the train. The railroad ran on tidal time: high seas allowed the steamers over the bars at the mouth of the river. When the steamers docked, the trains ran. Like me, she waited to hear the whistle blow through the tumbling air. And before her? Before the road came? My great-grandmother rode in the horse-drawn carriages that traveled on the hard packed sand of low tide. The wheels on the sand made the sound for silence, like *shhhh* pressed out between your teeth.

It comes to me; Jess has no sense of modern time. It's not built into her. She waits quietly for the surges in people, and she can feel them coming long before they arrive. So she never makes the nervous peremptory gestures that amount to deflection. Without meaning to, my daughter has become a woman who invites trouble in.

I round the point and head for the old rescue station. It's white shingle and green trim with low sloping eaves and dormer windows on the second floor, but the whole front of the ground floor is wide doors—for getting the boats out. We came here often when Jess was small, still small enough to settle between my legs and lean against me so that sitting, we formed a triangle within a triangle. I would rest my chin on the top of her silky head while her hands drummed out patterns on my knee caps. And we would imagine the horses that pulled the lifeboats through the breakers and the men who rowed the boats to the vessels foundering on the bars. Manes of foam whisked back by the wind and fore-locks flying, prows of foam pushed vertical against the top-side of a swell. And always, always, in Jess's stories every-one was saved.

I'm back at the motel within the hour, eight little board and batten cottages on the bay side in the tidal pastures. Like all the older buildings, the Getaway Motel faces the bay and not the road. Real news once came by water. I wait for something more immediate, the squeak of the mail box hinge, the trill of the telephone. But I know it won't come. Odds are, she's still riding that bus. The day will be over-cast and I'll doze through it hoping for her voice to break me from this spell. I watch in the flat light as the view bleaches into a band of white sky.

11

II.

I broke into my father's summer house on Lake Michigan with a butter knife. Not having ever met him, I wonder if he would find that amusing . . . like breaking into a bank safe with a hairpin. I find it amusing. He swept over his footsteps with great care, my father, the donor inseminator, the modern day mail order groom. The receptionist let slip that the good doctor was at his vacation home until Labor Day. I got here the day after, left the coastal waters of the Pacific Northwest for this inland sea of the Midwest. I rammed the butter knife in the window frame and edged all the way around and the old molding just crumbled away. I jimmied the pane but it wouldn't come, though I could feel it tilt inwards towards the house. So finally I let it fall inward, figuring better it fall inward then out, let the house enclose the noise, and it broke over the kitchen sink. I didn't know where to put the glass, but I found the entrance to the crawl space under the house, a wooden frame covered with chicken wire, so I pulled it away and set the glass under there piece by piece. I'll have to remember to remove it. What if next summer my father went crawling in to set rat traps or something and was disemboweled by a large shard. Terrible where the mind goes if you follow it.

As it happened, I cut my own knee, a piece I didn't see on the edge of the shiny metal sink. There's not much choice about where you put your legs entering head first through a window. You're horizontal so your only choice is to get a purchase on something or proceed chin first to the floor. And I can't afford any belly flops right now, I'm pregnant. So I got a fine gash on my knee about 3 inches long, arced like a beer bottle gash, the kind men wear on their cheeks. As I stumbled off to find the bathroom, it registered with me that I would be pleased later to have this scar. A memento, a curio of my own. And to leave a bloodstain or two on the hall carpet. Next year, he'd wonder how it happened, not remembering any major accidents with bacon grease or red wine, never suspecting it to be his own daughter's blood. What does he know about the permanence of blood, this man who made me with no intention of ever seeking me out?

I found him in the yearbook, University of Michigan, class of '69, year of my birth. After I told my mother I was keeping the baby, she began to help me; she knew that the donors were medical students. Common practice at that time. So it was her idea. There's a chance, she said. In those days, women were inseminated with fresh sperm so the procedure had to have taken place within two hours of ejaculation. All we had to do was find the closest medical school and call up the alumni association for the year books.

My face looks nothing like hers, though I have her hands and feet. Her restless craftworking hands, her calloused beach walking feet. But when a man looks in my face and falls in love, I don't know what it means, never sure what I see there myself.

The little house smelled of chill and cedar, like morning beach fog, also faintly spicy and sweet like sausage fat and maple syrup. In the bathroom, I could only find kids Band Aids with dinosaurs on them. I used damn near the whole box, crisscrossed, a sort of butterfly bandage. I rested on the toilet when I finished, soothed by the soft light coming in the opaque window above the bath. And I smelled something else then, warm like vanilla oil. Aftershave? My father's? I went back to the kitchen and pulled the checked curtains closed over the empty frame.

I have the yearbook with me. My father's face in a two inch square, third row down, one left of center. His face doesn't give away anything of his temperament, except perhaps a reticence to show any expression at all. The guy to his right is grinning like a sap, and the one on his left has his head tilted at an arrogant angle. Perhaps it says something that my father stares head-on, unsmiling, nothing self-congratulatory, no pretension there. I fixed on his face in a matter of seconds, once I'd gotten to the right page. I handed it to my mother, and she did the same. I found him so fast it was scary, but you can always find yourself on the page faster than your friends. The resemblance was that powerful. My mother thought I should double-check so I went to Angie's house and asked her. Do you think any of these people look like me? She didn't hesitate. Yeah, this man. Same man.

I'm lucky to have found this picture of him as a young man. Age might have distorted his features, but there he was, the lean young planes of his face exactly like my own, a chin like the butt-end of an anvil and the blunt Irish version of a Roman nose, a long Celtic face with eyes downwards tilting and a mouth made for hurt. I can't tell from the picture whether he has my hair, red as a copper pot and wavy.

Take your pick of fathers. The father who loved me unfailingly and would have understood my everything had he only known where to find me? Or the father who failed to love me and understood nothing of the nothing where he'd abandoned me?

I propped the book open on the bookcase with a beach stone I found beside the back door, presumably a door jamb. I wanted this young man to watch me move around in his house, as though I were now playing out some uncomfortable, cast-off second thought he might have had years ago, when I was only a gathering density in my mother's womb. *What if she tries to find me years later, what if I come home one day and find her in my house.* His mind plays out these modestly middle-class, midwestern, medical student dreams of townhouses and lake cottages, and I am some vague charcoal-hued shape moving through it. His little, tiny, two inch face is twenty-four-years old, but I speak in the present tense. The future dwells in the past. I'm here looking for it.

The cottage is olive green with a rust red trim, which sounds ugly, but it's not if you think of marigolds, which are the flowers planted in the sandy soil all around the house. A stand of birch and maple separate the cottage from the neighbor's to the south, supple trees that can take the winds rolling directly off the great lake. Beyond the house to the north, the graveled road ends on a bluff. The front of the cottage is sliding glass doors and a porch big enough for a picnic table. A long set of weathered grey stairs leads directly off the porch down to the shore.

The beach has been enclosed in a wooden frame; it's the

same for the neighboring houses and their beaches. I guess otherwise they would wash away. From above they look like adult-sized sandboxes.

The remnants of previous jetties are made of logs, not boards, and look like old fences submerged. The Macpherson jetty is warped, bucked up at the center. A couple of slats are missing from the middle, making a child-sized door frame to the lake. At least, this evening, it was child-sized; by morning, it might require a bellycrawl. I imagine children going in and out that door the day long, forgetting the drift of high tide toward afternoon and hitting their foreheads where before they had run through. Dinosaur Band Aids. Grandchildren. The sky turned the color of an apricot freshly broken open and the water was as violet as blown glass. Yes, I tell myself, like all the summers before, these are the sunsets we love. But there is no we; there are no summers before. These are not my memories. They are someone else's.

The cottage decor tells me something about my father that makes me like him. He finds luxury wearying. Luxury not only has to be maintained; it demands appreciation. The place is simple. I imagine that it is his, in other words, his wife has decorated the house in town but this is the trade-off. Old Naugahyde La-Z-Boy recliners, a nondescript tweedy couch, a mirror framed in the shape of a wooden ship's wheel over the fireplace, and on the walls those faintly colored paintings of famous landmarks that look like they were made with a 69 cent sponge—the Eiffel Tower and Westminster Abbey in thin gold, gilt frames—a blue afghan in the couch corner and a Hudson Bay blanket over a wicker rocker, round rag rugs on the floor in mallard duck colors. He'd like my mother's motel.

III.

This morning, there's a rim of fog over the water and above the coastal mountains. The sky above is a slender oval of blue. In another month, the afternoons won't be sunny. The fog will seal off that blue oval like an eyelid shutting for sleep. I hear the rumble of laundry machines on the other side of the wall. The maids sit on the washers above the cement floor and smoke, talking about which man will turn his life around and which man won't. Their conversations always dwell longer on the man that won't. I shuffle through reservation forms for the day's arrivals, then set them aside. The old Smith Corona Electric vibrates the pens in the jar on the desk when I flip the switch. An incriminating hum.

Jessica has been gone for three days. She is forcing me to know her father in the only way she can. If I write her letters, I have nowhere to send them. She presumes feelings of loss on his part, or of a vague haunting at least. Now I'm the one who doesn't know where she is. A chill comes with autumn and the lowering sun throws each branch and stone into sharp relief.

Alone, I dread the coming of winter. Seven a.m. winter light is white, fibrous as rice paper. We were always up together. My new-born daughter smelled like pepper tree leaves. There was no horizon line. Nothing to separate us. Not the night or the day, all gray, all gray and together. The sun when she came was like mother of pearl encased in lead caming. The days were swaddled in soft cotton, pale receiving blankets. I prayed to remember the soft time together against the time to come when she would hate me. In the early evening, while she was napping, I had a ritual. Outside it was raining. I filled the bath, closed the door to the lit hallway, opened the other to the dusk blue room and lit a candle. Let blue meet gold and water thunder. I was sound and color in there alone. I turned to flesh when Jess cried for me.

I had her to bind myself to myself—for the same reason that a woman will try to bind a man by keeping a baby or another will abort the child of a man she loves in a savage irrevocable action so she can't go back. Acts of salvation. I gave birth to her but she saved me. That is her terrible responsibility to love. I can't undo that with words. Even my actions to free her only bind her back to me with gratitude, or its replacement, resentment. She had to leave in fury in order to leave at all—the adrenalin pumped autonomy of anger. It's not that she fears my being alone. She knows I am good at it, too good at it, and she wants to prove me wrong, wants me to feel it as an affliction not a free choice. She may well succeed. All morning, I have memories of who I was before she was born.

Mr. Ramirez, the principal, poked his head inside the classroom door while we were singing counting songs. *Let's go riding in an elevator. 1st floor, 2nd floor, 3rd floor. Down, Down, Down.* I motioned to my aide and she took my place as they began the next one. He smiled at the children who were craning their heads around but his eyes were flat as a matt finish when he turned them to me. "Nellie, could you come to my office after the last bell?"

Maybe it was the Mooney child again. Her mother on a winning streak in Reno. The teenage sitter's parents had taken the girl in for a week last time. Or someone had called Child Protective Services. Perhaps this time Alejandro's parents were unable to get back over the border without their papers. Or maybe it was an outbreak of lice. My head was singing a lullaby to my heart, a looping melody to go round and round on, but Mr. Ramirez's look made me feel like a corpse laid out on a marble slab—so cold, blue and bare.

I never took a last look at homeroom seven. But I can still see the model city we made, cereal boxes covered in construction paper: high rises with yellow window squares, all the lights turned up bright and heads and hands inside waving out. My adult's view is nearly aerial. That's the city I remember leaving. And I still hear the sweet, bright chime of their voices, loud on flat notes like the clanging of cans, some child unabashedly in or out of tune on each note. *One lonely bird sitting in a tree, she was so lonely didn't want to*

be; So she flew away, over the sea. And brought back a
friend to live in the tree. Two lonely birds sitting in a tree .
. . Impossibly sweet. All of them doomed to self-conscious
gestures someday.

In Mr. Ramirez's office, I tried to laugh off his suggestion; instead I heard the screeching that air makes drawn
over a hummock in the throat. On Monday, my class was
told I was sick, too sick to finish out the school year.
One of my student's fathers had seen me at the movies,
holding hands with Julia. I tried to make the principal, Mr.
Ramirez, believe that we were just two women offering
each other comfort: Myself, a widow, friend and counsel,
Julia just divorced. He sat back in his chair appearing to listen, but he was only waiting. He wanted to humiliate me
with my own lie, to get even for all the compliments on
appearance he once paid me. The child's father had followed us to the parking lot, where we kissed goodnight. A
kiss like children imitating movie stars, experimentation. I
was the lesbian suitor, idealized beyond possibility. She was
waiting for me to be the catalyst, for the test tube to fill full
of silver vapor.

I never became Julia's lover. I still missed Monique.
And Julia told me about her childhood games with other
girls. *I'll close my eyes and you be Matthew.* She still
wanted that with me, to believe the kiss of a woman was
rehearsal for the right man. Or more impossible still, she
wanted a woman's love to compensate for the inadequacy
of her husband's, to be perfect, unblemished. She wanted
me to be the seducer with telepathic hands.

Monique had a voice that sang words. A voice for a picnic. She said "summah" instead of "summer." Her New
Orleans Creole accent sometimes made *oy* of *er*—nothing
like the exaggerated drawl of Vivian Leigh—so that she
would say General Poyshing for General Pershing, the
same vowel as *soyez* and *voyez.* Her skin was pale as a
Spaniard's but her thick hair had a tight wave and made a
wedge off the back of her head and her green eyes were
limned by lines of brown and silver as though there were
two other colors beneath the lens. She was another scholar-

18

ship girl in Ann Arbor, pre-med to my elementary ed. We liked the rhyme. She told me she'd renounced Catholicism to accept a moment of grace. It ran in her family: to be either alcoholic and Catholic, or sober and renounced. I'd never met a girl who took herself more seriously than the pursuit of a man, who always talked about serious things but fed them into the furnace of her humor. I told her the religion in my family was work, that my father happened to be Lutheran because his Swedish forbearers were, but what we really worshipped was their work. Just as with Jesus, we could never suffer as much as they did, though we could certainly keep trying.

Like Monique's father, my father would have shelled out ten or twenty grand to give me a wedding, but the college money was reserved for the boys, who could bring the improvement in themselves home. Girls were the ones who really left home, pitted by rice and baby pearls. I went to my father's lumberyard for the first time when I was eight-years-old. He was building me a playhouse with a pine panel finished interior. I sat in the slope of a propeller blade as big around as our car while the forklifts jacked their loads around me. I could have watched the cranes all day: gears and levers, the lurches of machinery, cables triangulating towards their targets, the huge steel hooks descending, the lumber swinging up and over, dwarfed in the distance so that it looked almost like paper wrapped parcels, then the slosh of the barges taking the weight and the clank of the suddenly slack line. A forklift operator moved piles of roof tiles on palettes. The curved tiles seemed to slump as the weight shifted towards the back of the machine. My father returned with a white bread sandwich, which we ate together. Then we stood at the center of the propeller and he hoisted me to his hip so we could see together. I relished his touch and the sound of his voice. He could wax eloquent about the way things worked.

Our lunchtime conversation had tapped his word reservoir dry and he drove me home in silence. A man comforted by the sounds of engines, who in everyday life spoke only what might be heard shouted over them.

I read my way through childhood. A.B. Guthrie's *The Way West* and *The Big Sky, The Travels of Jamie*

McPheeters, Rolvaag's Giants in the Earth. There had to be words for what people felt while they worked, even if they weren't much spoken at my house. I remember my mother's voice in the kitchen floating up the stairwell. She and Carson's mother were canning, pickling, preserving, always putting something up, always putting up. *That child lives in a book. I swear, the last time I read a whole book was on vacation.* Reading was a luxury indulged, like childhood. It was understood that time would take it from me, when I married and ran a household of my own.

I left Michigan when Jessica was six months old, a heavyweight baby who sat wherever I put her and toppled over whenever she reached for something. It was the last time I would cross the Great Plains on my way to Washington state. I was going home to see my father who had had the first of his heart attacks and portioned out the lumberyards in a will I had yet to read. Even before he died, my brothers whispered about buying me out. Family traitor. I had proof of it in my arms. They wished me luck when I bought the motel though I know they said under their breaths, she's going to need it.

On the way home, I stayed over a night in Monique's suburban Chicago home and met her husband Paul. Monique and I hadn't seen each other in three years, since graduation. We were all paying off student loans. The interior of the house was completely incongruous with its tidy, middle-class exterior: rattan furniture, batiqued pillows, apple crates for books cases, posters tacked everywhere, Maxfield Parish in sublime light and M.C. Escher with his ad infinitum perspectives. The white guy afro was in, Dylan with his Rainbow hair and Rob Tyner of the MC5 in granny glasses.

Monique and I drank Thunder's Mouth tea, stole a few moments together before Paul came home. We constructed the story I tried out on him, the story I was supposed to take home and proffer as a peace offering to my brothers. We granted paternity to Carson, who was dead anyway. When I think of Carson, I think of the years as children that we were lined up and marched—his slender head bobbing in front of me—then the roll call to Vietnam that didn't include me and the request for attendance that killed him. In a crowd, I still look up ahead of me as though I might see him. In 1969, I was grieving, and the lie felt like a tribute. Carson should have been Jess's father. According to Monique, my brothers wouldn't mind the lie if it would make me normal. So when her husband Paul asked me all those questions about "my husband's" regiment and his maneuvers, I was ready with answers. I simply gave him the news of Carson's death, as sent to me in the clippings from my mother. "Paul," Monique pleaded, when he asked about the wounds. "I can't help it," he answered, "I was a medic."

My sadness at their house was real. In the kitchen, they moved around each other at a calculated distance, like naval officers of different rank in the galley of a ship. At dinner, Paul performed surgery on his steak, disengaging meat from bone, and although very attentive, his rhetorical questions formed a kind of examination: "Half a cup only? Tired so early? Still breast-feeding?" The doctor through and through. I played the part of the nostalgic college roommate. We told him half-truths and looked at each other over our wine glass rims when we tipped our heads back. We told him about the college apartment, shaped like a T, the living room and kitchen then a bedroom on either side. My boyfriend, Stuart, who claimed he took a wrong turn one night and went to bed with Monique. The next night, he came back to mine and it was her turn to listen and cry.

"Didn't you hate each other?" Paul asked, incredulous. Yes, we did, we did for awhile, but we were so taken in by his terrible misfortune—loving us both. Remember, you had to have a boyfriend in those days. It was bad enough to be serious scholarship girls. We had a bond: terror of him choosing one over the other. This was what we told Paul, laughing as we told it. But I remembered how it had made perfect sense that either one of us alone was inadequate. Hadn't we always felt it? We feared we were the surviving species of an otherwise extinct line, and we knew, we *knew* there were girls out there with all the glorious features of adaptation built in, something their mothers had given them along the evolutionary trail. At night I cried to hear Stuart and Monique, not because he'd broken my heart, but because she made the sounds of real pleasure I'd never made. Her cries burst into the darkness of my sleep with the suddenness of a night bird, Monique whose cries had a melody.

"So how did it end? How did you get rid of this schmuck?" Paul was insistent once our hilarity had ebbed. After about a week, Stuart couldn't come over one night. Maybe he had to do some studying. Maybe he was tired. *His pecker was petered!* Paul roared. We giggled wildly.

We told him something about the end of Stuart, nothing about the beginning of us. I studied Monique's exquisite, expressive, unpretty face across the table. Her mouth was no longer sensuous because it was held in place by tension, one lip stacked upon the other. In conversation, I used to prick her and console her just to see the passage of pain to pleasure on her mouth. We ushered at the campus symphony performances. She wasn't ashamed the night I cried openly, and after awhile she set her flashlight on the floor and took my hand. It wasn't the music that moved me, nor the grandness—coattails, chandeliers, clapping—it was the man who turned pages for the pianist, the two together. One leaning into sound, his shoulders rising with the surge till it was all he breathed, and the other uncurling the paper so tenderly, with such apprehension of disturbance and such care for continuance. We made love like that, she and I.

I suspect Paul would still consider such emotions an indulgence. And maybe Monique lives a life too tired for them, now that she too is a full doctor. We failed finally at Christmas cards. Emotional triage. They talked about it at the table. For the parents of the malformed children who were under her charge in the hospital, she felt a vigilant pain, but the rest—colleagues, neighbors, relatives—were relegated to being abstract case histories, medical or social problems when she could get to them.

I couldn't do what she was doing unless emergency required that kind of courage from me. Wave upon wave of the cursed, the incurable, the maimed, the frightened, the scarred, the panicked, the undeserving. Monique had gone under, stolid as a mountain beneath the surface of the sea. All that evening, I sent signals like a sonar and when a reverberation came back to me felt relieved. But she was able to smile because I remembered her smiling. The evening together laughing was possible as a part of her past, not her future.

I didn't like Paul's stupid flirting. He admired the moon and stars airbrushed onto my sweatshirt. He consulted with Monique about the planet. "Is it Jupiter or is it Venus?" She walked past with an armload of dishes. "Ah, there's Venus," he said, flipping up my sweatshirt. He seemed pleased that I stared hard into his eyes, haughty and assessing. I still wanted to like him. If he would have touched Monique, just once, I could have laughed and thrown an arm around him, as though we also had a nostalgia to renew between us. Monique pretended to take no notice of this flirting, or in fact didn't. For a moment, I pitied him. He already lived in the kitchen of her life. If he slipped out the back door one night, she would bake bread not to notice. Each day he tried leaving a little more in hopes that she would notice.

After dinner, he held Jessica in his arms and when milk foam burbled from her mouth, he tipped her back like a glass of beer he could prevent from overflowing. "Here," I said, "she's got to get it out," taking her and mopping madly at the curds on his shoulder with a cloth diaper. Monique was laughing and so was I, but Paul's face had closed on a downward glance. She called to him as he went into the other room. "It was funny, you know, don't take it that way." He called back from the kitchen. "I'm making a drink, anyone else?" Thereafter, he excluded himself from our conversation. His laughter was confined to wryness and sarcasm. This open-palmed pleasure was the foolishness of girls, and he'd have none of it. The nostalgic roommate would be gone soon enough.

That night I made Jessica a bed in a wicker laundry basket and slept on the covered porch off the kitchen. The stove light was on and the shadows of the blinds threw slats of black across my face. I'd been asleep at least an hour when

I woke to see Paul standing over me, laying another blanket on top of me. His face in solitude was softened and kind. I reached my hand up to him. I don't know why—to be thankful, to be cozy, to pat him. The waking state is always that of a child; we ask the world to make us safe. His expression changed suddenly. He smiled quick and pained as if he had just taken a splinter in his foot. When he leaned over, it was not to take my hand. He kissed me on the mouth with his mouth open. A flick of tongue and I turned away. His expression was at once fright and rage. He didn't know what to make of the woman's face barred in shadow. He wanted to pry the slats apart with his hands and have me out, have himself out . . . no telling on whose side the bars lay. His retreat was hasty, angry, and silent.

In the morning, Monique brought me orange juice and sat on the bed with the baby in her arms. Jessica rooted around on the flannel yoke of Monique's nightgown for an opening, making sounds like a little warthog as she searched for a nipple in fistfuls of flannel. We traded orange juice and baby, then I got Jess settled and sucking. Monique looked over her shoulder then down at her tawny feet, spreading and unspreading her toes as though she had something to be embarrassed about. We were both watching the doorway. There was so little time. Then she spoke.

"I still wonder if I'm gay, Nellie. Do you?"

Her expression was so totally earnest, I winced inwardly. I would have liked to touch her, but I didn't want it mis-construed as taking advantage of the moment. I had an urge to put Jessica back in her arms so she could feel the comfort of warm nestling against her, but the baby was firmly latched onto me. The urge to comfort nearly over-rode the need for a careful answer.

"If you're asking whether I still love you, I do. But I don't wonder anymore whether I'm gay or not," I answered.

"Well, you have a reason to be."

"Does one need a reason?" I asked gently.

"No, I didn't mean that. It came out wrong." She shook her head.

"Don't you think some people just fall in love with a person and gender is secondary?"

"Maybe, that would explain loving you then Paul."

She took my hand off the coverlet, pressed it between her own. "My Nellie Isabelle." She liked to use my combined names—her soft S and piquant L rounding the sounds till they lingered in her mouth. We smiled softly in separate directions. I knew how difficult it was for her to make declarative statements about love; for her it shifted the meaning from feeling to vow with betrayal implicit. She was grateful I created an opening for indirect expression.

"Will you love a man again?" she asked after a moment.

I balked at the question. I felt a sudden urge to pack. I had to laugh at myself, at the way Monique always pinned me with my own weighty generalizations. I did laugh.

"Monique, when you ask that question, my impulse is to lie . . . it's such a reflex by now. I've faked it for the outside world so often."

"But I'm asking you really."

"Well, I loved Carson, so it's possible. I can't say. The thought of hurting Jessica might prevent me. She has no father and then suddenly I have a lover?"

"You never know, maybe he could be a father to her."

I withdrew my hand and put both my arms around Jessica. My voice was strident. "Why are you trying to make me so happily ever after with a man? Would it be reassuring to you?"

"You don't like Paul, do you?"

"I'm not predisposed to like him, but it doesn't have much to do with him, does it?"

"He has his tender side."

"I know." I answered without thinking, but she wasn't watching my face or she would have seen the admission there that she was working scrupulously to avoid—his flirting, his midnight excursion.

"He understands my ambition." She sounded more plaintive than defensive. There were sounds in the kitchen of cupboards opening and water running.

"What about your passion?" I whispered.

She shrugged, but it was almost a jerk or a twitch, and she wouldn't look at me.

"Passion looks to me like unnecessary pain, like self-absorption, like selfishness. I can't help how I've changed. I'm going to make coffee."

That morning was the first time I knew I wanted to go home. That I wanted to be away from Monique's questions as much as she wanted to be away from mine. In the bathroom at her house, soaping my hands with a scallop-shaped pink soap, I wanted to go home. But I wasn't thinking of the places I drive by now, every afternoon on my run to town: the old sloped houses with power lines looping from roof corner to roof corner and back across the railroad tracks; the trailer parks that look as much like tin cans washed up shoreside as anything else, plastic butterflies in increasing sizes alongside their doors; the 1920's bungalows converted into motels, teeny weeny novelties to unpack the kids into, 12 coats of paint thickened to their shingles; the downtown converted into a Coney Island of Amusement Park rides and Ye Olde Everything Stores with pull taffy machines and brass sailboats, and the original cannery now a restaurant full of kites. The tourists congregate downtown to buy post-cards and T-shirts signifying their trip to a beach they never seem to spend any time on. No, it wasn't this. With the small pink soap in my hands, I remembered the purple snap-dragons that grow in the wild wheat grass of the dunes. They fit on my fingers when I was a child. Thumb and fore-finger of both hands. I made their velvet and scarlet skins kiss.

IV.

On the bus ride out here, I thought about how it's possible to set out on a journey in America *not* to discover oneself and succeed. From on-ramp to off-ramp, from Burger King to Burger King, Motel Six to Super Eight, Arby's, Bob's, Wendy's, Denny's, every place the same place. Why not be a chain-outlet person? Go home with the first person to mistake me for somebody they know. My father's already in trouble. I don't want him to be like anybody else.

Tomorrow I'll call him, I say to myself as I sink into sleep. I've been at his cottage nearly a week, wrapped head to toe in a gauze of exhaustion. This afternoon lightening and rain. The sky is the color and density of steel wool. The resistance of the air to my body moving through it makes me feel my own shape outlined in sweat. The lawns release fertilizer vapors in the humidity. Fireflies skitter over the dusk-darkened green, up into the black fingered maples. Then it comes, blue heat lightening sheeting across the lake. I stay awake for that.

The baby skims off my energy like cream. I don't ask myself where I'll be to have the baby. I nap. Mid-morning. Mid-afternoon. On the tweedy couch with the Hudson Bay Blanket over me. I don't ask myself what I would do if anything went wrong. Or maybe I do. Pick up the phone like anyone else, but it goes no further than that. I've missed the last train of thought to pull into the station. I can just keep up with feeding myself. My appetite is immortal. A sandwich on a plate looks like a party hors d'oeuvre.

Last night, I felt a slow tightening above my pubic bone, which drew upwards all the way to my breast bone. I felt muscles I never knew I had, crisscrossing like a basket woven around my baby. I went to the index of my *Complete Pregnancy* book. Don't ask me why they can get away with that title. It makes me shudder now to think of any pregnancy less than complete. I feel like my body is a giant cargo plane revving its engines on the runway. I am terrified the signal from the tower will be given too soon. I try not to but I think about my mother, like this, by herself and pregnant with me. And how do you feel after the hours and years of rocking and singing lullabies in that tone that teaches about desires never met, never satisfied. *When you wake you shall have all the pretty little horses.* And dressing the little body day after day and paint sets and play dough and cotton ball bunnies and Christmas ornaments made of two pound dough babies tilting your tree. If I called her, we could talk about the baby: a whole new safe subject. What a relief that would be to her. I don't know how anyone finds anything in that book in the middle of the night. *Rehearsal contractions . . . . Braxton Hicks.* Was he the guy who discovered them like the first man on the moon? As far as I'm concerned the entire index could come under the heading "Fears." I don't like flipping around in that book. It keeps falling open to those gruesome photographs. Women getting double chins trying to look down there so hard and grimacing to see themselves distended in lurid color—cracked red and wrinkled black—about to shred like wet tissue paper while the caption reads: "The baby's skin is still crinkled up like a rose petal before it has opened," when you can see its skin has the texture of an old turkey wattle.

I found a family photo album under a bunch of paperback mystery novels and crossword puzzle workbooks. It's incomplete, original intent abandoned. Pictures of the cottage from all four sides, east, west, north, and south. Then there's one with the three boys and their mother standing on the kitchen steps, but it's from too far away: four small white people squinting, standing in a line and decreasing in height like dry goods jars lined up on a counter: flour, sugar, coffee, tea. I'm glad my father is not in this one, the family shot. He's outside looking through a lens, like me. Then there are pictures of every room, all empty. The kitchen wallpaper is the same as it is now, yellow and white gingham. The bathroom is still pink. From the outside, the place doesn't look any different either. Maybe my father's wife had grand plans to remodel. "Before" pictures but no "after."

The boys are sitting around a large mixing bowl on the floor. The eldest has secured the bowl with his feet. The toddler is curling his toes as he sucks frosting from his fingers. The youngest is tracing over the glitter whorls in the linoleum with one chocolate coated finger. My mother has pictures of me like this, straddling a bowl with frosting on my face.

I have to admit I don't like the pictures with my father's wife in them, but I make myself look. She's sitting on the beach in a one piece suit, broad-striped as a beach chair, and she's wearing a straw hat with a brim that curls up ridiculously. But I'm not being unkind. I can see by her smile that she's terribly self-conscious, even about having her picture taken, and that her self-consciousness is her charm. She's so modestly genuine, she could never be stylish, not for a minute, and she knows it. A pained admission to the camera's eye. The baby in her lap looks toward the water, unaware of her embarrassment.

There are endless pictures of the boys on the beach, digging dog-style, dripping sand castles into spires and turrets, scampering in and out of the little doorway. Then there's one of my father at twilight, sitting on a log with his arms around the shoulders of the son who looks like me, the baby newly on his feet. The baby stands with his heels together, his stout legs bowed from locking his knees. He's clutching a fold of pant fabric with one hand while the other rests at his side, slightly curled. The image arrests me.The fisting and unfisting hands of babies. It's easy for me to cry, wishing I were the one guarded in the enclosure of my father's arms. It's easy for me to idealize him; we have no family history of ambivalence.

Pictures of a white-muzzled family dog with a beach umbrella clenched between his stubby teeth. Suddenly, I know there's no one that would look at this album and sob but me. A person might look at my mother's photo album and wonder the obvious: Where is the father? Who is this other woman? A relative? Of course it's Angie, my other mother. But whatever they thought, they'd sit back, fold their hands and say: Well the child looks happy enough. She was. She's digging trenches, dog-paddling to shore, smiling while her mother pushes her around in a wheelbarrow. She's doing all the things these children are doing. I could glue most of the pictures together in the same book and you'd think it was the same beach. That would be one way to have a family get-together. Maybe there's something to it. Why his was the sperm that took.

In this one, they're building balsa wood gliders at the kitchen table. There are cookies on a platter. The glider decals are collected in a shoe box. My father and his first son are using a nail file to deepen an insert slit. The other boy stands behind my father's chair rubbing his eye. It's taking too long for anything to happen. The youngest is holding onto the table ledge, back for another cookie. My father's face is in profile. Back lit, it looks less harsh, less bullet shaped. Long, like the patient profile of the crescent moon in nursery rhymes. Hey Diddle Diddle. I recognize something in the softening. It's only love that makes me pretty. My face has the charm of a dark urn by candlelight. I lengthen the flame.

My father stands in a field of sand and scrub grass flying a model airplane on a string. His youngest son, the one who looks like me, stands knee-high beside him. A series of snapshots take the plane full circle. My father keeps a fierce eye on the plane, even when it flies across the sun. He has stopped trying to make out what his son is saying. He is flying the plane. He has gone to the sky. Upwind, the sound bursts about the boy's ears; downwind, it fades to a buzz. He is not looking at the plane. He is looking for a way out of the panic circumscribed by noise. The father squints; the boy winces. Upwind, downwind. My ears ring from the picture. Is this too what I missed?

I search the closets upstairs and find an old playpen, toys in a laundry basket. A string of wooden ducks made of thread spools with wings like little paddles that go round when you pull the string. Six miniature milk bottles that fit into a carrying crate with a handle. A ballasted bird with a convex underside; she'll jingle but she won't tip over. I sit on the floor remembering when my hands fit the shapes of these things.

My pre-school was in a converted brick warehouse. Huge windows began six feet above rows of cubbies and coathooks. I was happy at my projects: gluing macaroni to kleenex boxes, rolling marbles over blobs of paint in a box top, shaping little bears out of cinnamon and applesauce that the teacher later baked. And dreamily I looked up at those windows, where because I couldn't see their trunks, the branches of the trees seemed to float by on a current of cumulus clouds.

It must have been around Christmas time. We were cutting chains of angels in construction paper and trying to peel the points of stick-on stars out whole. Our mommies were the chain of angels that wound around our days. Our mommies dropped us off and kissed us goodbye and picked us up and kissed us hello, and our teachers were altogether mommy-like and Jesus in the picture belonged to all the children. I went to hang my vinyl apron on the wall and I saw a man standing beside the alphabet chart, and a boy named Courtney disengaging from the group to run to him. *Poppa, you came to get me!* And the man went down on one knee and gathered him up and carried him legs dangling to collect their things from the cubby. My mother told me my poppa was with God, that he died in the war being brave, and she showed me a picture in a rosewood frame. I wanted to make angels wearing pants. I know now the picture was of Carson, her high school sweetheart who died in Vietnam. Even though she lied to me, her tears were real.

Daily, my mother filled my pockets with raisins and dried apricots. Once I snuck my hamster out of his cage in the kitchen and put him in the pocket of my pea coat. By recess, he'd eaten through the sweetened lining, and I could feel him bunching his little body to sleep along the hemline. At home, my mother laughed as she stripped the seams to find him. He was groggy from dehydration but she didn't scold me. At dinner, we had contests to see who could suck up the longest noodle. Her laughter and mine. I hear it still buffeting against the bones of my skull. This last year we've laughed together so seldom. I long to forgive her as one locked in a cell longs to find a loose brick, fingers tracing the seams of mortar in the dark, over and over.

When I nap, I dream of fish. The moon is full and the tide is low and the grunion are running. Thousands of them. Slivers of silver on the sand. I have to say the tongue twister, over and over. *Slivers of silver on the sand.* And I have to rake them all up. Another wave comes in shimmering with fish, and faster than I can rake, they mate.

I wake to the rhythmic lapping of Lake Michigan, not the crushing growl of the Pacific. The image of the fish still twisting from light to dark. I remember the first time I made love in the neon light of the motel sign, the room turning off and on, the man a black body in a strip of light. Blink, off, blink, on. Each time I imagined it was a different man—always trying to create a memory I don't have. My mother lay on a paper covered table with her knees up and a plastic straw inside of her while the sperm of many sloshed in and sloshed out. When I was eight and we went to pick Aunt Becky up at the airport, I watched each man who disembarked, especially those with families to greet, though I didn't look at the families. I kept my eyes on each man's face and let it be the moment before he greeted me. Even if he was balding and stooped and untidy, I let my heart lilt a little so I would know how it felt.

The next morning, I wake early. It's six o'clock, the hour my mother usually rises. The shadows between the ripples on the water are silver. In the distance, red leaf maple, sumac, and birch cast color over the water though the still air has a sheen of black.

Nigel once asked me if my mother and I were close. We are and we aren't. Every statement I make about her has to be like that. She is and she isn't. We are and we aren't. I've longed all my life to feel one solid thing about her, even to disregard her as a pleasant boredom would be relief. She never apologized for anything without finding a way for me to apologize too. So I had to take my anger away with me again. At twelve, I would capture bees in a jar and then shake the jar and watch while they stung each other to death.

My mother's lies were high drama, scenes to make me weep. The poor Nellie stories. She told me Carson's parents lied about the funeral date because they couldn't bear the public shame of my illegitimacy. I used to picture her standing alone over the grave with me in her arms; it was always windy. She told me Carson's parents asked that I be christened. My Aunt Becky loaned my mother the family christening dress. That part's true. It was the one my grandfather was baptized in, layers of fine mesh linen and hand-crocheted collar and cuffs. She said they went to the church believing Carson's parents would come, but only my aunt was there to stand up with her. Then there's the story about Carson's brother who supposedly came to the motel and tried to seduce my mother. She told me he hung around after dinner, dropping big hints. *You must get lonely, a woman like you.* She knew he was there to snoop around and if he couldn't find something, create it, so they could bring charges of unfit mother against her.

For me, the stories had the strangeness of fairy tales or fables. My illustrated Aesop's showed a picture of a crane with its beak down a wolf's throat, dislodging a bone stuck crosswise. When I was seventeen, I got a long look down my mother's throat. Angie, who had just moved out, helped me find Carson's parents in the phone book. They told me he had died a year before I was born and offered to show me the death certificate. They were so sorry. Sorry I had a crazy mother? Sorry I wasn't his kid? I spent the rest of the summer with Angie. When I'm angry, the whole world isn't enough room for me.

As a child, I was happy to have two mothers. Angie was my gentle alternative. For as long as Angie lived with us, my mother and I had a truce that held. Later Angie told me things about my mother, and she helped me see how my mother's stories were metaphorically true, analogous to a memory or feeling she couldn't or wouldn't recount to me. My mother will always stand over Carson's grave with me in her arms asking him to make me his. She will never forgive my grandfather for refusing to love me. She will always be afraid of men.

I was nine or ten when Angie came along. My mom had put an ad in the paper for a motel maid. Angie walked into the Getaway—kept it short and straight—she hadn't worked in thirteen years. Angie's husband had been a football bookie who went crazy slowly. She said that was why she stayed so long. She'd fought leaving him with everything she had. I guess you can only do that once. Her husband had turned paranoid before she left. He tried to persuade her to walk around the house one way while he walked around the other way. Like a Bugs Bunny cartoon. And him with a gun. She made us laugh when she told it, though it wasn't funny. I think my mother liked her immediately.

That first Thanksgiving, we ground cranberries by hand, mixed them with orange rind and sugar. The rains came and the tree branches looked like black scratches against the sky and the light from the lamps inside appeared more gold with each day of lengthening darkness. We made sugar cookies for Christmas and stirred marmalade into our tea. If the toilet sang all afternoon out of key, who minded so long as it flushed? The frost bit into the ground and the great spider migration began. Angie would open the door shouting *Come all ye spiders!* We listened to Old English carols in Alfred Dellar's clarion tenor voice. *Here we come a wassailing upon a midnight clear, love and joy come to you and to you your loved ones too.* Yet I watched my mother closely. She would rest her hands from her task—curling the ribbon with the scissor's edge or twisting tissue paper into roses—and raise her eyes to the window, the sadness in her keening to a sound out of doors, the hard heels pounding in the rain towards our door.

When I was twelve Angie moved in with us, and I saw my mother in relief, a sharp form against billowy, blowsy, stone-washed Angie with her Tarot cards and her pulp novels. I saw the way my mother sized men up as they walked toward the vacancy sign: not their character but their physical prowess, as much as to say, this one I could out-run, this one I could scare with a little hysteria, this one wouldn't stop short of a knife blade. After making the assessment, she could afford to be friendly. Angie was always friendly, always acted as though she were just looking up from a 300 page paperback and the penultimate scene, but of course she would set it aside for you, because you were here and she was glad to see you.

My mother could only be nice to wrecked men, fore-closed men, men who drank resignation and flirted because it was in their nature not because they had a shred of expec-tation left. Jack was like that. Jack who ran the laundry ser-vice. When Nellie and Angie turned forty in the same sum-mer, he took them both sky diving. My mother said she felt the scenes of her past life flying out the back of her head like a deck of cards turning into an accordion and making terrible noise. Angie said she drifted, she drifted down onto the world like a child choosing to be born.

By high school, I knew they were lovers, though when I asked my mother she gave me their standard answer for public consumption. *We're business partners.* On my way out the door to a rehearsal of the school Christmas pageant, I sassed them and they laughed. *See you none-of-my-busi-ness partners later.* My mother could afford honesty prof-fered as humor; humor asks no direct questions.

After Angie began doing the books, the accusations started. My mother suspected Angie of stealing money, sending it to her daughter who was in rehab. *If I needed money for my daughter, wouldn't I ask? Your mother's so afraid of betrayal, she creates it.* I remembered all the anec-dotes of my mother's that used to irk me in the telling. Inconsequential and created for humor as they were, they all told the same tale. The plumber tried to gyp her, the mechanic tried to rip her, the traffic cop tried to bully her—gyp, rip, bully. But none of it happened, oh no, because she was far to clever, she saw it coming, she knew what to do. And if I knew the kind of pressure she was under, running the motel, if I knew . . . . (And wasn't it all for my sake in the end?) I sympathized to try to make her rethink it, to try to make her extend benefit of the doubt. But Angie was already packing. *Don't think this makes me happy,* my mother said.

Fuck you, I answered, *You don't want to be happy.*

Rise and shine. I rise all night in my father's house, like sourdough starter. On top of the refrigerator, there is a cookbook, its binding held together by strapping tape gone yellow. Recipes typed on tracing paper and two tattered newspaper articles fall out. *Sherry Party for Museum Patrons* by Maggie Nygren, Society Editor and a column entitled *Please Make Me a Better Worrier, God: A Woman's Considerations.* The book is full of color photographs, the flat gleaming color of grade school textbooks that makes every subject look like plastic. There's a chapter devoted to Leftovers that recommends Spaghetti Roll Ups: leftover canned spaghetti rolled up in a thin slice of ham. *Yum.* My mother has her mother's cookbooks, pots, pans, and jelly jars. With Angie, we made applesauce. How I loved the old devices—pushing the center of the apple onto the prongs of the peeler and watching the red ribbons spiral downward; or turning the adze shaped blade that pressed the mush through the ricer, and trapped the peels against the sides. With Angie there, my mother could let on to some of her hurts. *This is obscene!* she said one night, pointing to the chapter called "When He Carves" which included drawings of a pair of thick, stubby hands dancing around all variety of meat cuts. It was ghoulish—distinctly man hands disembodied but carving merrily. *I'm going to rip it out,* my mother said. *Do it,* Angie answered, and she did.

I turn now to a picture of a root cellar with a big bin of potatoes and a sand pit for burying turnips, beets and rutabagas so they won't freeze. I try to imagine my grandmother in the picture of the root cellar, or in the picture of the kitchen with white steel cupboards and a big pan of bread rolls cooling beneath a sill where tomatoes have been lined up to ripen. These could have been her cookbooks, original copyright 1942. My mother seemed to always be angry at her, said she could have been a piano teacher or she could have been a librarian if she hadn't always been taking care of Him. But I liked my grandmother because she was calm and smelled of baking and swayed on her feet and hummed all the time.

My mother says she was never allowed to get ambitious about anything. Just when she was beginning to achieve mastery—debate team, drama, piano—she was hauled off to do something else so she'd be well-rounded. Wanting to be a lawyer, actor, concert musician; not realistic. It was a danger for a girl to cut herself off socially, to find absorption and intensity in pushing herself. My mother is still frustrated, and she doesn't think I'm serious enough. She wants me to go into some hard-core men's profession—electronics, architecture, industrial engineering—not anything as typically female as teaching or nursing.

The book advises: "When company comes at odd hours, don't be trite. Serve something that justifies your reputation as a smart hostess." Company picnics, company dinners, a new foreman. How many Liberty Bell Cookies did my grandmother bake, Deep Dish Peach Pies, Blueberry Drop Biscuits? My own mother could transfer crust into a pie dish from wax paper without so much as a fissure and press a perfectly fluted edge in record time. Baking pies conjures all the right associations, makes a woman safe, and she knew that when she baked them and took them to my school functions. But in the summer, she covered the garage door with butcher paper, so I could make mud prints with my whole body. My friends all wanted to come to my house. Buttock prints, hands and feet, we even made our heads into mudbrushes. My mother was the most fun.

Even as I say that about her I have to contradict it. The familiar boil of bile and dread in my intestines. Before Angie lived with us, there were days she didn't dress and the dogs slept in her bed, and I'd stay home to try and run the front desk so people wouldn't see her in that maroon velour house dress, unzipped and covered with dog hair. Beneath her eyes two blue half moons floated like boats, the marks of sleeping with her mascara on. I didn't know what depression was then. She was asleep when I left for school, and asleep in the afternoons when I came home. The maids took reservations in the morning, and I returned calls when I came in. I knew how to make my voice slow, melodious, and womanly.

She used to leave money under the butter dish and I got off the bus downtown to do the marketing. I shopped with a bitter heart, no one to care for me, and I bought whatever I wanted: Pop-Tarts, Spaghetti'O's, Captain Crunch, fruit rolls, canned pudding, beef jerky. When my mother appeared in the the doorway, I'd look up, guilty yet praying she'd be angry with me for doing such a dismal job of caring for myself. But she ate whatever she could find, pulled up a chair in front of a bowl of Sugar Pops. *Are you going to go to school today?* Her question was perfunctory; mine was unkind. *Are you going to get dressed today?* She brought her fist down onto the table. The spoons danced, the demons out between us now. *You look like your father. You act like your father.*

I'd threaten to leave forever, with each step toward the door making a proclamation. *I'm leaving. I'm going. I didn't ask to be born.*

Go then! she shouted. *I put you back where I found you! I quit!*

I hid in the garage once, where we had an old chest freezer, and I ate one popsicle after another listening to her scream my name. *Jess? Godamn you. Jess?!* My heart was hard as a peppercorn. I wanted to hear fear and repentance. The screen door slammed twice before I heard the slap of her slippers on the drive and the jangle of keys in her hand. I watched the steel wheels in the track over my head jerk towards me as she flung the garage door open. *There you are,* she said. Her arms were crossed, gripping the excess material of her sleeves, then I saw she was shaking. *Why didn't you come when I called?* But I was the one who bawled, trying to find words for the ways she used my love against me, fruit juice dripping down the front of my pajama top, my bare feet cramped and cold on the cement floor. *Get in the car.* My face streaming tears. *Please get in the car.* She fired on all eight cylinders of our Chevy Malibu with a terrific blast of gas, then shoved the fan and heat levers forward. *I'm sorry. I'm so sorry, sweetheart. But you mustn't say those things. Your father left and never came back. I couldn't stand it again.* She would apologize but somehow it was always me hurting her. The fact of my existence. Born to hurt others. That's who I am. *I'd do anything for you. You know that. I'd die for you.* I heard proclamations of need not loyalty. There was something she wanted

THE SPERM DONOR'S DAUGHTER

said. Not that I would die for her. That I would be born for her.

After I found out my father was a semen donor, she never blamed my bad behavior on him again. Though for three years I went to great lengths to make her do so. No, in her mind, this donor was merely a catalyst, something as scentless and innocuous as water poured over a seed. Sometimes I love her for this, for claiming all my badness. *Do you think my father had depressions or rages?* I'd ask. *Do you need so much to know? You come by it honestly enough on this side.* So I'd take another tack. *Do you think he's a journalist or a historian and that's why I love to read so much?* But she refused to imagine him into being with me. *Well I'm the only one in my family that devoured books, and no one ever told me where I got it. Remember I was a teacher, you know?* Sometimes I hate her for this, for seeing herself as a blueprint for me, giving me no room to surprise her, for making me hers through and through. I refused to discredit or dismiss him, though I knew no qualities of his to defend.

Every man I ever loved left me, I figured insemination was a shortcut. It's not the kind of thing I hope you'll under-stand someday, I hope you'll never understand. Carson's death was a leave-taking I didn't recover from. I told you he was your father so you'd have a good story to grow up on. But he'd proved to be a disappointment too. He wouldn't marry her before he left for the war, at least that's what she says. Sometimes I say to myself: disappointment is my father.

I don't consider my story so odd. My friend Jackie's dad was sent to jail for selling cocaine and he used to beat up on her mother. Jackie has some memories of her father. One time her parents were fighting and her mother ran to lock herself in the bathroom but her father was too fast. He shoved her backwards into a tile shower stall where she fell and cracked her head. When he went to jail, Jackie's grand-father helped out. He mowed the lawn and paid the bill when the utilities company was about to shut the power off. After the divorce, her mother married her ex-husband's father. Now her grandfather is her step-father. How would you like to explain that? This is my grand-step-father? I say my father was gone by the time I was born. *Ever hear from him again?* No, it's like he vanished into thin air. Kids like Jackie envy my situation.

There are snapshots of Carson and my mother standing on a stone bridge in the wind. Carson was chubby, crew-cut, wearing chinos, a windbreaker, a big metal watch. My mother was wearing a heavy loden coat, the kind with a hood and wood toggles. She was closer to the edge of the snapshot frame, but he had his arm clamped around her. My mother was pulling hair out of her mouth and laughing at the same time. Carson was looking straight at the camera and smiling, as if to say, "This is the first frame of forever." I don't know what it's like to lose love, only that most of my friends' parents lost it anyway, and that's not an observation my mother ever factors into her loss total.

I didn't do well my last year of high school, which effectively cut me out of the scholarship scene and all my mom's hopes. What a relief to be cut loose. Jackie's brother was hyperkinetic and had bottles full of ritalin. We ate most of his prescription that year. God knows how he got by. I had to recite the elements chart in chemistry, fill in the blanks. Mrs Wallia was Pakistani and her bindi became the red center of my whirlpool. *Strontium, barium, uranium, red dot.*

I could see the names in my head but they looked like pieces of clothing in a washer, a centrifuge that spun around the red dot on her forehead. *Oxygen, Hydrogen, Nitrogen, red dot. Try again, concentrate Jessica.* She asked me if I felt well, placed her pretty hand on my forehead. If she'd placed it on my chest, she would have heard my heart skipping like a scratched record.

My English teacher, Mrs. Sundquist, devised tests for the kinds of cocktail parties she had to endure, the official functions. *Match the quotes to the correct authors.* Quoting snippets to display erudition while eating hors d'oeuvres was obviously important to her. Not a damn for what I thought of geese as rapists, immortals descending, Zeus and Danaë. Wasn't I the product of an immortal lust? I daydreamed constantly. Mrs. Sundquist would turn from the board in her dark gabardine skirt, hand prints of chalk on her hips. I imagined my mother, bent over and kicking, unable to refuse an immortal. Her hubris had earmarked her for such a lesson in humility. Oh I was vicious, and full of longing too, sometimes a sorrowing Persephone returned to her mother from the underworld.

What of the hubris I inherited? I tore up Mrs. Sundquist's final exam. It was satisfying to hear that slow ripping in the silence, to do it slowly so that it destroyed each student's concentration; the girls dared not look up, only glanced at me sideways. "Sheez," one boy said, shaking his head. Gina Giannini passed me a note: "Jesus loves you anyway." I slipped one back to her: "I am the miracle of immaculate conception." By then the whole room had paused, and Mrs. Sundquist was glaring at me with the obvious question, so I told her that what she'd seen and heard was in fact what I'd done. Torn up the exam. "Jessica, Are you going crazy?" For once, it was not a question in patronizing tones while she withheld the answer, not rhetorical either. All heads snapped up. "Yes, Mrs. Sundquist."

"Then you may be excused."

I smoked a cigarette under the cement stairwell and cursed that brick Taj Mahal with its textbooks full of prickless statues. *Chipped off.* It became a code expression between Jackie and me. I see myself, standing in my school issue wool kilt, a bit tilted back—the spine of a child, the breasts of a woman. *Every man dreams of saddle shoes.* I dreamed of myself that way . . . saddle shoes over my head, bucking for a brooding storm. My mother would later fight it out with the principal's office, earning no points with them for saying they couldn't keep up with my restless intelligence. *The class spends three months covering one novel with those bloody mimeographed discussion sheets while my daughter is reading three novels a week. How does Mrs. Sundquist expect to keep her interest?*

I admit I made a practice of being intractable. It seemed important. I thought the world was ending. I warded off most everybody with my bad case of weltshmerz. I prided myself on knowing what the word meant.

Mr. Flotre was one of those unfortunate men with the affliction of having a fanny, set off the more by the short man's propensity for wearing cowboy boots. He taught Algebra the way he coached basketball—barking all the time and throwing erasers, reserving himself for the few stars. He began each hour with the hardest problems on the board—inside of fifteen minutes successfully humiliating the peons, goading those who kept up at all, and separating out his A-team for the rest of the hour. His reputation outside of school was for the tequila bottle, and his voice sounded like he'd swallowed a few worms—hoarse and nasal at the same time.

I could manage the word problems with their variables for X and Y, but without the words the numbers and letters looked like cuneiform or Sanskrit, some language rubbed off of a stone. *Zero doesn't divide into infinity at all but infinity divides into zero endlessly.* When Mr. Flotre said things like that I never heard the rest of the hour. I wondered what practices the people of such a language used to ritualize it. What they carved or built to signify it. All my nothing and not being in that room still a part of something and forever. Whatever knowledge I gained he had no part in, and I refused to take the final exam. Never mind the afternoons I cut out with the juvey boys to go condo-hot-tub-hopping, I didn't consider myself unteachable. Mr. Flotre took me out behind the modular after giving the class problems to work on. Ours was of a different nature.

"You might pass the exam if you took it."

He feared my candor. "But you haven't taught me anything."

"I've explained the problems over and over."

"Yes, but always the same way."

"Look, I'm trying to be a nice guy here."

"No, you're not. You don't want administration to hear why I refused to take the final."

He snorted, scoffed before swinging his rear around on his boot heel. "I'm not worried about my standing here, but you ought to be."

I didn't follow him back in, and he left me staring at the whole green playing field in front of me. *Standing where?* The chain link hood over the pitcher's mound looked like a net holding me from the sky.

When my mother called Mr. Flotre, he told her that he was terribly busy. *Of course you're busy,* she said, *I expect you to be busy.* But she was battle weary by then, decided to let me go to junior college and bang out my own consequences.

I became man-eating to keep my mother at a distance. In a man-slather. So I could say, *Look, I get along with all these men. It wasn't the men. It was you.* The summer I turned eighteen, I slept with every man at the motel who'd have me. Ever seen those check-out time questionnaires that come with their own envelope? *Tell us how we're pleasing you.* What could she do? Close the motel?

She used to wait up under the porch light swirling with insects. I could smell the smoke of her cigarettes as I crunched across the drive.

They won't make you happy.

What makes you think you look so happy?

Maybe you'll be luckier than me.

I intend to find out. I'm not the bellhop of love you know, I don't have to drag your Samsonite up and down stairs for the rest of my life.

Well, don't get pregnant. Unless you want to be a suit-case.

One morning as she was putting away my laundry, she found the crumpled tube of Ortho-Gynol nesting in my underwear. I watched from the bed. She picked it up between her fingers the way you would a dead moth, by its wings. *Getting a lot of mileage out of this, I see.* Then she dropped it back in and closed the drawer.

My mother had her little ways of getting even . . . all the little ways she needed me. Even in high school when I tried having an honest-to-god boyfriend. If she had a compliment for one of them, it also turned out to be a slight. Oh, she took them into her confidence, and they liked her. Nellie.

Nothing like their mothers. Thin, rangy, smoking, leaning over the motel front desk, offering them her cigarettes. Still sexy too, the way her front teeth push forward like a flock of birds in V-formation, that permanent, indeterminate sort of smile her lips have to close over to extinguish. And the boys swaggered a bit in her presence: woman with a motel. It was almost as good as being in a bar, and they couldn't go to bars yet. Oh, she genuinely enjoyed them too, even as she found ways to make them know they were exchangeable, disposable. *Jeremy, I think I like you. I think you might be alright. Maybe the finest man to come along.* And sometime later his mind would jog the implicit words into the blank her smile had cleared: *finest to come along* (after all the others). *Tim, you're the first man around here who can fix things, not just jerry-rig 'em* (among the many who've tried). And all the while she told them how much she and I were alike, how much she understood her daughter's needs and so granted total freedom. Until finally the fellow himself had to wonder why the others had failed. And the more I tried to make myself different, the more mystery my mother accrued.

On two occasions, my mother had to resort to the photo albums because the boys simply weren't bright enough for her technique to succeed. She patted the couch cushions to signal the most comfortable spot for him to wait while I finished dressing. The albums she chose were full of promdates, beach kissing, camping trips, boyfriends in shape and size as different as a batch of blocks. Sometimes I found my desire for men all dried up, and in its place, the tart sweet taste of my mother's love like the dart of a thorn on my tongue.

V.

One week, seven days, no phone call, no letter, nothing from Jess. I've started talking to myself as I move through the day. *I talk to myself because I like to hear a sane person think.* That's what my mother used to say. I want a way to explain things to Jess that won't sound like I'm blaming my decisions on bad advice. She wants to hold me accountable. Somehow what I've done is worse than unplanned single parenthood, marriages scattered right and left like demolition derby hulks. I spared her that but she spares me nothing. Why is it so much more threatening that I should *choose* to be a single mother, well-prepared for it I might add. I guess divorce, desertion, and death are preferable; I could claim victimhood and cast myself in some softer light. But I was raised not to speak of what I endured, that was part of triumphing over it. Later, in the Seventies, we newly lesbian read Mary Daly, theological maverick of our collective: *Beyond God the Father.* I remember the joke: *Madonna, Madonna, why are you crying? Answer: I wanted a girl.* Well I have one and she is unforgiving as flint. So much for female nurturance. *Lizzie Borden took an axe and gave her mother forty whacks. When she saw what she had done, she gave her father forty-one.* Lucky mom. You get it first . . .

There's a distinction, I realize, between losing a father and never having one. Have I tampered with God's creation? Will she be the only one in class to read Frankenstein as a family history?

No father. For my mother it was tantamount to saying there is no god. My daughter wants to break me down into simple wrong and right. She wants to break me down like an interrogator. Alright then. Hear my confession in your bulb-bright room. Hear it all. How my father viewed your creation as immoral because I'd combined the double whammies of masturbation and adultery. I wanted to speak the truth even though I was counseled by the doctor to secrecy. My father was dying and I told him, because he *knew* me; he knew I'd been raped and he knew I'd loved Carson. I'd been away so long I'd forgotten the heroic family code of pretending. I violated it. My mother treated me as though I'd killed him with my news. My brothers joined her. They pee a fine mist, that lot. Isn't it all so sad? How do I make Jess believe that I haven't constructed this to exonerate myself? I don't want pity. I gave her the happy story so she woudn't have to pity me.

What does Jess really want to know? I used to dream I carried the child of my attacker and delivered it dead through my mouth, spitting out the black blood clots and smiling because I'd won and he'd never enter me again. I'm like a man who refers to the baby in his wife's belly as "it" because he can't bear to say the word baby. I can't bear to use the word "father." Does she want to know how it felt years later when a doctor told me that postmortem sperm retrieval is possible. Yes, sperm production is the last bodily function to cease in a man. I shouldn't wonder that Jess is so driven to find him. Spermatazoa. Little vehicle of him that once swam to me, little summary in a squiggle. Does she want to know now that I dreamt of Carson's body torn open the way you can pull apart a ripe peach and me in the mud with my seventy-nine cent eyedropper and his last words delivered in black and white like a World War II movie: *You have to do it.*

It hurt me—like disloyalty to Carson—when she rejected the story I'd raised her on. She can't see me as a child with him on the harvest beach, not far from the mud flats and oyster beds. Low tide, the eel grass lying flat, the clams squirting into the heat at intervals, old couples in canvas hats carrying shovels and digging. We searched for the barnacled siphons of horse clams protruding through the sand. Though they look like sea anemones, when you start digging they're feet long. They squirt and pull away from you as fast as you can dig. It's no wonder they're called horse clams; their siphons wrinkled, reminiscent, just the right size. We shrieked and taunted each other. *You grab it! No, you grab it!* The tip retracting like a barnacled foreskin, the muscular strength of the thing a match for us, and the whole situation some strange archetypal mix-up, the way dreams patch images upon each other and reverse them— being pulled into a hole by a penis in reverse. Then a kind of delivery, pulling forth a two or three pound clam: blue brown in its shell, milky and opalescent at its rim. How shyly we looked at each other over our prize. After Carson died, I would dream the memories, and it was hard not to believe I hadn't conceived in my dreams.

Jess wants me to admit I need someone other than her. And I want her to admit that the others can't replace me. If she had to sleep with an airplane load of men, (a boat full, a motel's worth!), I'm glad actually that I could provide them. Of course she did it right here thinking only to make me mad but it gave me the chance to watch over her. I finally told her one night she couldn't be the whore of healing. After Vietnam, my whole generation of men were wounded, whether they went over or not. I spent hours with J.T. who used to threaten suicide regularly, playing Russian roulette on the phone. I could hear the click of the hammer when he pulled the trigger. Then his sister told me he was just flicking a Bic lighter into the receiver. You tell me which was worse—his suicidal tendencies or his sick humor—since you think my pessimism is so depressing.

I understand more than she thinks. In high school, I had a best friend, Christine. We saw each other off to college, made sure of it. But when Christine came home for Christmas, she set about systematically seducing not only my brother but also Carson, home from boot camp. And seduce them she did, quite successfully. Perhaps in her distorted way, she simply wanted to join my family. Of course I felt like a fire hydrant a dog had marked on his morning rounds. And Christine ran up my phone bill with her weeping, her remorse. A drinking problem . . . . She didn't know herself that she was going to do it. The latter seems true enough but I think it takes an act of will to stay that drunk all weekend—drunkeness with stamina, with intent. Years later, I wondered if Christine hadn't simply wanted to sleep with me. Less as an act of homoeroticism than cannibalism through sexuality. The cannibal eats the strong heart of the warrior whose strength he intends to have. But I'm uncharitable here. Easier to leap to anger than fall in sorrow, always my flaw. And I still sorrow over Christine, an adopted child whose sister (also adopted) wound up in an asylum for life after which the parents who'd chosen Christine cast her off. Where Christine didn't have blood ties, perhaps she tried to forge them through the primacy of sex. Or she wanted a sister-love, a mother-love that was unconditional and she chose to test mine.

So my little bird, my daughter, you seek to bind a brother to you, or is it a father? Or would you like to eat their hearts for strength? My love seems to offer you so little.

VI.

When I first found out I was pregnant, I felt like I'd been hijacked . . . someone else was flying the plane, telling me where to land in nine months while down below I could still make out my home town. In the afternoon, the exhaustion comes. I sit in one of the porch chairs with the afghan over me and the weak fall sun on my face. I can barely blink. Stillness. I feel like a lizard waiting for an insect to land on the end of its nose. This morning the lake was absolutely clear. I could see the sand bars, gold bands beneath cerulean blue; now the lake is chalky and pale. Muted like me.

I doze to the lapping of the waves and the pattering of birch leaves, half-conscious, floating in the sounds. Monarch butterflies move lightly on the breeze. These waking dreams are of last year's men, each one a vignette for a goodbye unsaid. These are the truer goodbyes, the images stored up against the mornings of departure. With our clothes off, the mannerisms of self-protection are so obvious. I think my ass is too big so I'm always backing out of rooms or walking sideways. You have to pretend you don't notice their inward flinch even though they know you're pretending; then they're willing to tell you things. You're the one they can talk to.

I wanted to know about the hurt that men hide. There was something about each of those men, even if they were rough with me or condescending or painfully grateful or remembering someone else they still loved. The man who worked the septic lines had carpal tunnel in both wrists. His hands would go numb in the middle of the night and he would wake up and shake them back to life again. Too many years of picking strawberries, picking fish, shucking oysters, and packing meat. He made crude jokes afterwards. "I always say, don't sweat the petty things, pet the sweaty things." The newly-divorced maritime engineer couldn't manage making love but could laugh at himself: "This rubber needs suspenders," he said. He cooked me blueberry pancakes . . .as if he had to make up for it, and I wished for awhile that he would come back. The fat-boy trucker from

Kansas constantly apologized for his "great plains manners," and profusely thanked me for his first blow job. He made trucking sound like mythology: "There wasn't a thimble full of blue sky in that semi loaded with beans." The ex-logger who limped and waited for the Department of Labor and Industry to settle his claim called his mother and his sisters when he got out of bed with me—to tell them what he would have for dinner. The retired teacher on vacation with his botany books and his telescope recited for me— Shakespearean sonnets, his favorite parts of *Moby Dick*. After his fifth scotch he'd forget and recite them again, always the same passages. The man who ran a salvage yard for boat parts showed me his wallet's worth of snap shots: wives and children strewn around the state like confetti.

I want to know about man hurt—so I can identify it when I find my father—so I'll know if any of his has to do with me. The vignettes of men in my mind don't make sense as goodbye scenes, not really. They don't carry the self-conscious poignancy of movies or novels, but they are a way for me to say goodbye now, each one a distillate of personality. A certain open-armed gesture, curls kinked with sweat at the back of a neck, squared off palms, thick eyebrows that tangled in my own until they looked like shredded wheat the morning after. In the end, the images are with me not as memories culled and kept, but like the imprint of shells on a bank of clay. This year, at twenty, I am a thousand years older, holding hunks of clay in my hands and examining the imprint of trilobites. There's no salt smell here, but still, I dream of home. And there's only one man that I miss.

I see Nigel, the first time he pulled up at the hotel in his dark green Alfa Romeo. The girl with him is wearing a paisley scarf tied under her chin, the way women looked in 1950s French movies. I saw her as a girl even though I didn't see myself as one—nineteen-years-old, pushing a towel cart across the parking lot. I think now that Nigel loved me in part because I *could* leave him; I have the strength for it. He probably already has a new sports car girl . . . one who will whine and wheedle when his affections stray, his attentions diminish. Always it's a girl, though he's nearly forty now.

Yes, we girls are so hungry for the world, measured and poured in Nigel's hands like medicine from a bottle, just the right dose, for just the right effect. But my mother raised me to believe that men weren't there even when you thought they were—that was the moment most to beware of, most likely for them to disappear.

Nigel has a hard incisive look; you wouldn't want to have to ask him to repeat directions a second time. His eyes have the lines of a woodcut, angular, because the line of the lids extends beyond the actual eye. He has high color in a man's way, blood in his cheeks but not a girl's flush—the sign of arrogance in a man with an outwardly calm manner, restraint, not placidity.

He has to unfold his long body like a beach chair in order to get out of the car. He takes the girl's hand and she lets him lead her up the path to the motel office as though she wouldn't have known where to go otherwise. The next morning, when I go to make up their beds, there are marks on the wall behind the bed posts where the plaster has given way. When I finish cleaning, I go to get some Dap and a spatula from the tool shed, to fill the divots in the wall. I see them coming in from the beach, heading for the car. He opens the door for her and as she slides into the seat, he straightens and looks at me. The look conducts a charge like metal; after the initial jolt, it begins to sting. I don't turn away because I want to know why we recognize each other. In a dark room, I would recognize his breathing. That's how I feel. He collects and catalogs hurt too, but it makes him angry at himself that he does it. Then they pull out of the lot and the girl turns her head to see who I am. Just the maid in a man's flannel shirt. She knots the scarf under her neck.

I'm alone in the office when he comes back the next weekend, by himself. He explains that he's here meeting with potential investors for a fish farming operation, doing site evaluation.

I'm unimpressed. "Do you want a room?" I ask as insolently as possible.

He smiles, slow and wise and wan. "Yes, I can provide the girls myself. You don't act the small town part, do you?"

"I'm not from here, not entirely," I say as I slide the forms across the counter towards him.

He glances at the black plastic ashtray full of my mother's lip-marked butts and asks, "Mind if I smoke?"

"Go up in flames, for all I care." He laughs and looks at me like he isn't going away before I admit that I like him.

Where the mouth of the Columbia River gapes widest, a thousand boats have gone down. That's where I take him. There are lumpen, grass covered islands half a mile long in the river. Flocks of birds rise from the reeds, fall into the reeds. Underwater, the islands become sand bars. We climb in silence to the lighthouse that stands on the humpbacked promontory of the cape. I resist the urge to ask him any questions about himself. I imagine that he expects questions; that his answers are all script. I know nothing yet of the way his mind plays. He smokes a pipe and the tobacco smells like cognac and chocolate. The smell of luxury, travel, perpetual discontent. I am determined to observe more about him than he would have me know, and I think he senses it. I think it gives him a kind of pleasure.

I act the tour guide. I tell him about the first ship bearing a great glass bell in its hold, the one that went down in the 1840s. And about the gradeschool stories of a beacon that burned beneath the breakers. But I stop there. My mind always fills in the picture with a convocation of willowy gnawed shapes in a half-light dancing and sharks skimming between. My mother peopled the sea with immortals in an effort to turn me from a childish preoccupation with decay and dying—Poseidon and his trident, Bottocelli's Venus in her shell—but I only mixed the images indiscriminately, forming a court of the deep where immortals held forth and the dead talked until their jaws fell away. When we come to the sharp escarpment that faces south, we stand awhile.

"Bones and shells roll across them together," he says, nodding towards the sandbars. I back into him awkwardly as I step away from the edge.

He leans down and makes the scary wind-noise that children make. *Weeeeee—yeeeeew.* Long and sing-song against my neck. I turn to run up the hill, and the wind lifts my hair, whips strands of it into his mouth.

The lighthouse extends skyward from a platform of fenced-in flat, while all around ascent or declivity immobilizes hardy picnicers who watch their thermos bottles fly off cliffside and their hard boiled eggs tumble into tangles of madrone and red cedar. "I love slants," I shout, my words torn in streamers from my mouth. But he has heard me. He comes up close alongside me then, saying, "Show me how you love," and he watches my face for the telltale hesitation he hopes to find. I falter but it doesn't embarass me because I'm no innocent. I make a gift of it. I smile when I see how he enjoys this brief admission of attraction. Then I invite him to lie in the grass with me beneath the lighthouse. He doesn't hesitate at all.

With our feet downhill and our heads tilted back, the huge black and white cylinder tilts against the sky as though we had caught the moment just before its fall from the cliff and crescendo below. Then we lie with our feet uphill, and the blood pouring down into our heads swells our eyelids, and the turret tilts towards us, filling the whole frame of our view as though it were falling right onto us. We listen to the boats sounding the first and fifth of a chord and buoy bells between, the notes lengthening in the moist air like the slowing of my heart. Gusts of wind travel up the cliff and fold over the headland, mixing the stench of the cormorant rookeries with the sweetness of new grass. Acid and salt, that which has passed into the gullet alive and died on the way down, the smell is sharp and merciless as first desire.

Nigel's apartment in Los Angeles is grand, parquet floors and built-in china cabinets with beveled glass doors and a cupola for a breakfast nook. The windows are old glass, hand blown, you can tell because they shimmer with rainbows like bubble solution stretched across a frame—corn syrup mixed with dish soap. His bed is built into the ledge of a bay window. As Nigel's hands stroked me, I followed the swirls of color in the window and listened to the harbor chimes and the air loud as sails luffing.

When I first came there it was a cloudy afternoon, after

a fancy lunch, full of wine. His blue-beret tipped barward and his lips tipped towards me. His bite for mine, we fed each other. *What would our love smell like? Calmata olives, tangy and sun-dried? Sea bass wrapped in grape leaves? Rabbit in a cognac cream?* But once at his place I turned shy. I could hear voices in the street, syllables pattering like rain in a pot. He uncorked a stubborn bottle and I couldn't watch as he rocked the cork out though I heard the slippery sound. I began my little bit of lying, because I thought that too had to be done. *I should go back now.* He laughed. *Before there is no going back? I like to watch you teeter at the brink. You said you loved slants.* Then I laughed. I'd wanted all my life to feel something inevitable and random at once. A moment to yoke contraries, and here it was. My hands moved across the table like leaves blowing along a road, hands out walking alone. He stroked my fingers and the soft web of skin between them, and he sat at the table not suggesting anything but letting me see his shyness, his ferocity, his need for mercy.

It was getting away from me, this moment we were studying carefully, its predecessors pushing it aside. I had to tell him about my collection of hurt ones, how I learned to be the maiden drawing water from the well, to bring up in my bucket this need to *do it like a man.* Soon they were all the same: men I overpowered and then tended to and pretended not to know about. What a weight. The tired ballad of bed. And if I made a little associative leap, if I let my eyes change color, let myself rhyme sounds or sucks, well it was all a shock they tried to be up for, to please me, and it wasn't a leap at all, it was my invitation, my lead, and them waiting upon it, until I'd have given my soul for an unexpected free fall.

Nigel turned my hands over in his lap; he rubbed the hearts of my palms and made my fingers curl. Without his eyes on my face, I never could have said what had been the matter for so long. He whispered into the shade that had crept over the room. The house plants made a lace of leaves on one wall. Someone in the building was baking custard, the resplendent smell of carmelized sugar. The windows were turning blue. *You may regret things in your life, but*

*don't ever apologize for it. Not to anyone. You want to play
the instrument for every sound it will make, there's nothing
wrong with that. You're easily disappointed; I won't disap-
point you.*

I felt that he wouldn't. Later I learned why. He is a man
who is fascinated by women, who has submitted himself
wholly to this fascination. His knowledge is vast, but unlike
most men who want only to know that they are good, he
wants to know women, he wants to breathe in their exhala-
tions and live on it. His is the seduction of the willing
novice. To each woman, he apprentices himself utterly, does
not for a moment apply the likes or dislikes of any woman
who has come before her. Because it's for you, all for you.
He makes himself a slave to your desire, and therein lies the
attractive strength—*I make myself a slave to your desire.*

On the day I remembered all this, I was wearing a
sweater I found in the bottom drawer of the dresser desig-
nated mine. Black cashmere with an embroidered name tag
sewn in: Constance Delacroix. I laughed when I found it,
imagine, a name tag as though she were going to camp.
Now I suspect she was a foreigner. When I read her name,
I said it aloud, I elongated the second vowel until my voice
got husky, elongated it into absolute beseechment.
Constonnnnnnce. The sweater was slack on me. Her fatness
must have been a delicious luxury, a softness yielding to
heaven.

It was not the first thing belonging to a woman that I had
found. A lipstick: tea rose. I was wearing that too, as we lay
together, listening to the sounds of the corner market—
casual greetings, children counting change for candy—the
sounds overlapping like wet pieces of paper. He didn't
notice the sweater or the lipstick. He stroked me and I
stroked the cashmere. The next woman would obliterate
me. *Constonnnnnnce, where are you?* Fleetingly, I longed
to go to her.

But that first time in his apartment, the blue twilight
washed down the walls, and the smell of whole milk and
eggs baking filled the hallways. What if I can't feel? I asked
him. What if I can't feel? He asked me if I liked my hair
brushed. If I liked my back scrubbed. If I liked warm soup

on my tongue. I put my arms around him then and began to laugh. Of course I can feel, I told him, it's only when I should start to feel more, that I begin to feel less, until it diminishes down to nothing. Usually the man comes then.

He said I must tell him, I must describe each sensation with each touch, so that he could be like the shadow I cast, never losing me. I kissed him on the cheeks, on the forehead, and we left our shoes under the table toppled upon each other. But I couldn't write on the air with my feelings; I couldn't give that much away yet. He told me then I must only say warm, warmer, warmest. Then he stroked my face, the smooth underside of my jaw, the death opening at the base of my throat, the bony hollows of my collarbone, the incline of my breastbone. Stroking to the sound of the little waves that rush up to the sand but sink in before they can recede. *Warm . . .warmer . . .warmest.*

Warm . . .warmer . . .warmest . . . . I said it.

I stayed with him in L.A. and began by doing temporary secretarial work in the garment industry. Nigel bought me the clothes he thought women go to work in, dove grey skirts with slits that didn't allow me to walk in my normal stride, and I had to learn to take short, mincing steps, and sit at my desk slightly knock-kneed. Real silk blouses with covered buttons and choir boy collars. Was I so sexy even my buttons must be covered? Nigel said I was and that he would begin his seduction by stripping the buttons with an an exacto knife.

I got offered a job with a company called Saylor that made designer knockoffs in much cheaper fabrics. At first, I worked for the regional vice president of the western division, Mr. Tobin, a gruff, comforting man who wore a suit the way an overstuffed chair does its upholstery, pulled taut and tacked down with brass tacks, in his case, cufflinks and tie pin. He had eyes like buttonhole slits and a reputation for ruthless business. But he treated me with an offhand affection because I was not cowed by him.

When I was still there on a temporary basis, my job was mostly to open his mail and stack it in piles for the executive secretary away on vacation, whose head was probably still ringing from four phone lines. I offered to do more but no one could be bothered to show me. So I made no pretense of being busy with their paperwork. Mr. Tobin seemed to like that. One lunch hour, he offered me the mini-TV he kept in his office, but I told him I liked to read. One afternoon, I'd set down my copy of *The Second Sex* by Simone de Beauvoir to answer the phone. *Hello, can you be helped?* That was just how it came out. Mr. Tobin passed my desk, then he saw the book. "It's not what you think," I called out as he was closing the door. He held it open a crack, for just a moment. "Sure, sure," he said still chuckling. I didn't bother to explain. If Mr. Tobin wanted to think someone could write a 500 page porno novel about a second of sex, let him. Maybe it got me the job.

I became a front line receptionist in the warehouse where the sales people showed the different lines to the buyers. The receptionist station was this twelve foot long half arc that faced the elevator bank where I sat with three other women answering phones and filling out requisition orders. Nigel had dressed me all wrong and they didn't like me. They wore sharply tailored magenta blazers with black skirts or checkered blouses over black skirts, with gathered waists and Victorian flounces to swish behind. Their smiles were brittle sugar as I took off my camel hair coat. Who did I think I was? Dressing like one of Mr. Tobin's college bound daughters. It wouldn't have helped to tell them I'd cleaned motel rooms all my life. I wouldn't have liked them any better if they'd liked me.

Nigel let me keep all my money. He's a mechanical engineer, specialty robotics, and he travels to tool and die companies to design swinging arms, automated drill bits, conveyer systems. Everything with an automatic shut off and restart. He said I should go to a real college. He also said he wanted me to go to Europe with him in the spring when he would travel on business. He wanted me to be free to go with him. He also wanted me to be free to go. From the beginning, I was saving against that day. But I didn't mind that I didn't like the job. My mother raised me on women's biographies. I knew that to be an interesting woman, I had to have an education in heartbreak. I had to fail in love to absolve myself for other things, though I don't know what these other things are yet, only I feel the portent of them like a lead keel, an everyday weight. I was determined that my readiness to leave him, my preparation and my vigilance, would mean *not* having to leave. Sometimes I got up and went walking in the middle of the night; I wanted him to startle in the dark alone. I wanted him to know how ready I was; how alike we were in that way. I used to think that Nigel wanted to be known . . . by someone . . . by me.

The last time I saw Nigel, he drove out to the motel one more time, and I had him meet me in that same room where we'd made love in the beginning. Except it was morning and the beach light was white as the insides of the curtains that trapped it against the window sill. I remember thinking, this beach light is white as a newborn, as the undersides of your arms where I will go seeking our youth when we are old, and still find it. But Nigel was old already, and I didn't know it, if being old means to foreclose on possibility.

Too much regret, not enough time, never enough money, should have, could have, would have . . . . We were a duet on dissonance. He tocked off losses on his fingers while my voice buoyed up all the things to look forward to. He did not, in this mood, want to look forward at all. He was begging the world not to require anything of him—the way children determine to stay in their rooms forever. He had locked up inside. I dreaded anger even as I felt heat at the roots of my hair. Odd I should remember the day I snuck into his basement while he was at work: geraniums set to winter years ago now yellow on a tin table, the wicker chair with peeled legs, stacks of black drum cases like cake boxes and guitar cases too, leaning like women waiting to dance.

I don't know why I thought there would be a grand gesture of reconciliation. I needed him to dream and he was being careful not to dream. The quiet ones in families endure, they make it look easy. They go so far toward secret lives that dreams become a means of hoarding safety. He had come to give me all his reasons why I should go through with an abortion—something *he* wouldn't have to do—while I would be left anyway, empty and scarred. It was clear to me then, I would have left him if I had gone through with an abortion. Threatening to be done with me if I didn't do it wasn't much leverage. There's a sound the heart makes just like dry twigs snapping. And I could look at him without recognition, blankly, as though a magic coat of paint had been rolled right over the wall where we once cast shadows.

And yet his body dreamed with mine. I did an experiment one night as he slept—erect and pressed into the small of my back. I would contract my inside muscles, imperceptible, you would think, but for each contraction, he would pulse in return. I smiled in the dark. I still believe he loves me.

After he left, I tried to feel what it must be like to be him. When I was Nigel, the sunset didn't move me because I could tell a story of a much more beautiful one in a strange and far away place. When I was Nigel, I told the story to a young woman who'd never been anywhere, but my words didn't paint pictures for her eyes to see, only rated sunsets, and reminded her of what she hadn't seen. It was easy to convince myself that I was mysterious, unknowable even. Though the buoy lights at dusk were the color of blue roses and the sky was an orange exhalation soft as the sound of breathing, it didn't move me when I was him. I still found a way to be lonely.

I remember another time, early on, when Nigel wasn't yet trying to rationalize us out of existence. But the distance between now and then is like trying to travel backwards on the sound of a train horn after it has passed—the Doppler Shift—when the velocity of approach suddenly changes to the velocity of recession.

The bird we came upon in the sand was black and dull as charcoal dust on pulp paper. The news of an oil tanker spilling in the straits to the north had thinned the summer crowds. Nigel was the one capable of observation. The bird was not covered with oil, its undersides were green with kelp bloom, young with full flying feathers but not flying now, only blinking when we spoke and sleeping between.

"The oil is traveling south," Nigel said, stroking the bird's back. It stood up then and pitched forward onto its beak. "But I don't think it's here yet. Maybe he got storm-tossed all night."

"Maybe he's just in shock," I added hopefully, thinking of all the birds dying somewhere to the north and the headlines that daily gauged harm to humans and reassured. Sometimes I believe all humans should die; I believe it because part of me wants it, a consensus of recognition forced upon us at last, but too late and too bad our own indifference came to kill us off at last. When I was in the sixth grade, I was asked to write a saying for the school year book. I turned in "Man was not the exception, he was the mistake." They chose someone else to write about "always growing, ever learning," some sot. I fault myself for grandiose thoughts. You'd think I could stay with the situation for five minutes . . . in the sand on my knees with the blinking bird before us.

"C'mon," Nigel said quietly, "we can at least give the little guy a chance."

I didn't tell him my feelings because supposedly it's not very adult to insist on wondering why we create so much sadness. I followed him and he carried the bird like an offering cupped in his hands as we walked away from the dog tracks on the hard packed sand and the four-wheelers speeding by. It was in our power to give it at least a chance, if nothing more. I watched him walk into the heavy sand dunes, shifting a bit side to side on his slender legs and I was thankful that he was a man who dropped to his knees before small creatures and I was determined that we would not create any sadness between us. Before we left, I looked from the bird to Nigel. As he opened his hands to settle the bird in the sand, he winced. For a moment it was easy to forget that he's older than me. All the baby birds he'd rescued to shoe box nests as a boy and fed with eyedroppers, and when they died anyway, he had this same face, the one I discover in my memory over and over again and always with relief.

VII.

After a few years, it was easy to forget that I was lying to Jessica. Not because I'm devious, it's a trait learned in families. After a few generations, a little elaboration can become accepted record. And anyway memory flows like igneous rock, folding over images indiscriminately. I came across a photo when I was packing my parents' things for the estate sale. I'm standing in a field of daffodils at two or three wearing a pale blue dress with a row of ducks appliqued along the hemline. My mother is kneeling beside me, one hand on the back of my head. I feel her pleasure at our dressed up occasion, the warmth of her hand on the nape of my neck, our mutual admiration of my new white shoes. This is the totality of my memory for that age. But it's not in fact a memory; it's a photo my mother kept for years in an oval frame on her high boy bureau. It shocked me to realize the photo had inserted itself as memory, become memory.

Only when I was with my brothers and their wives did I have to feel the lie, because they knew about the insemination. I couldn't follow through with the fabrication I'd tried out at Monique's. Carson's parents were alive and well. Anyway, I cast myself out of the family when I sold off my shares in the lumber company, bought the motel, moved to the coast. I can't live in their sub-divided days, new bird-less neighborhoods with deathly quiet views. We saw each other less and less after my father died and exonerated each other too readily. *They could call if they wanted. You could . . . They could . . . .* The question of Jessica's legitimacy was present in the family watchfulness. There were too many adults intent upon her. The other children felt it too. *Does Jessie have a fever? Is she sick?*

My father never touched Jess. Maybe that would have changed if he'd lasted past her first birthday, at least I like to think so. He built things for her, a cradle on wheels, a rocking chair—some way to contain her without having to touch her, a way to touch her but once removed. He'd made things with his hands all his life . . . but he could not put his hands to her, as though it would have been an admission of participation in my heinous deed. To him, she was worse than a bastard child; she was a mongrel or a mutt. And I tired of my brother's wives holding her in the kitchen and scrutinizing her features for family resemblance, disassembling her face as though she were one of those potato head dolls with snap-on noses and eyebrows. *What will you tell her when she gets older?*

I'll tell her her father was a generous man because he gave me his seed, because he knew how much I wanted her. But that isn't after all what I told her, when she was old enough to ask. The lies I told Jessica were the truth about how I felt, they were my only vehicle . . . and then it was so easy to forget that she wasn't Carson's child, so easy to see his face in hers.

I can't make my memories of Carson into a story for Jessica. I live by incompleteness, the unfinished narrative. She thinks I am incapable of loving a man when the truth is I love ceaselessly. I am like one of those ghosts that haunt highways because I don't know I've died and no one can tell me. To cut off love at the moment of absolute readiness is sudden death. Only the stories of the supernatural or freak occurrence have any bearing on who I am. Perhaps she could know by analogy. I'm thinking of the Swedish expedition to the North Pole at the turn of the century, three men in a hydrogen-gas balloon, how thirty-three years later their remains were found on a barren island amidst the ice and letters delivered at last to one man's fiancee.

In the way that dreams compress or suspend time, nothing has happened between the time he left and the moment she receives the letters. My memories are a reverie so powerful, I need to be slapped awake. The hands that hold the letters have aged, but not the heart that receives them. She sups with strangers, her own husband and children. Only banal exigency pulls her back in and presses familiarity upon her.

I know Jess went to her aunts and uncles after our blowout. And also to Angie. I'm sure they opened the files on me, relished the job. Jessica could have asked me herself, but she wanted to punish me. The untrustworthy mother. And punish me she did. It's not over yet. I remember those poison nights, walking the floor as though I were crunching glass beneath my boots. Like an actor trying out lines, countering their version with my version, version with version forever and ever amen. The whole family psycho-analyzing me, breezily finding reasons for things I'm still not sure I understand. I know I didn't want a father there for Jessica to love, their love complicated by my inability to love him, making each day a lack and a loss.

I called over to Angie's. Contrition wore my molars down. I asked Jessica polite questions about her plans and waited to provide counsel, as though it made all the sense in the world for her to drop out of community college and leave town with a man twice her age. Of course, Nigel now provided all her counsel; she needed none of mine. I shook his hand in the parking lot, then kissed both my daughter's cherry cheeks as I had her first day of school, inwardly begging the world to be kinder to her than I had known it to be. She was excited. She was laughing. Our truce was holding. She withheld her disapproval and I mine. We must have appeared to Nigel a pair of chums, my daughter and I. Ironic that. The whole scaffolding of lies she'd brought down resurrected in an instant to hold us up in his eyes: a mother to be admired, a daughter devoted. Or is that merely hopeful on my part? Everyone says I'm in denial. Shit, how do they think I would have gotten through a day after the rape? After Carson's death? After Monique's marriage? I'm all for denial if it enables you to function. Everyone thinks they can cure me of suffering; it's not a disease. Flush your damn pills. I don't want to dishonor my dead like that.

So how much Mom-bashing did Jessica do in his presence? Was Nigel merely playing along? I can imagine her impassioned invectives; it even moves me. I don't care now. My bargain was with the God who sends girls home—anything I might have said against Nigel would only have been perceived as more of my rapacious need to bind her in a pact between disabled women. *Come home darling and we'll hate men together.*

It hurts to make the noise of laughter. To be like me is

condemnation. She can't afford it. Will there be a day I can tell her the measure of my loss was the depth of my loving? And that there is nothing that could have guarded me against the loss. Nothing.

I'd been at the county fair all day, brushing horses, braiding manes, showing in the 4-H arena. My father was to pick me up at the exit by the livestock tent, when the tractor pull was over. A man his age opened the back of a van and asked me to give him a hand lifting a crated ewe. When he tossed me in after, I banged my head on the wheel well. He pulled the doors shut and trussed my hands right there in the bed of the van. What had anyone seen? A girl helping her father, loading her lamb. I could hear the roller coaster, the Ferris wheel, screams turning on a wheel; no one heard mine.

By the river where the man takes me, the cottonwood seeds float across the water on a warm wind. Old bait containers litter the beaches, bright orange salmon eggs glimmer in the shallows. I can still hear the screams of the children on the roller coaster at the Fairground, a sound pulled up and down the air. *Watch your step*, he says. Taking my hand to lead me up over logs and river wash, things I don't need help over. In the van, his thumbs had put marks on my neck shaped like clusters of grapes. The calloused ridges of his fingers are lined with black oil.

I see myself everywhere in the river. I will be a woman who comes up in a river. So this is the reason not to do . . . all those things. This is the reason and I know it now. The white limbs of logs lying lengthwise in the river are my fleshy reflection. The shine of jars along the bottom are my eyes looking up as he strangles me. Lures hooked to the bottom are my earrings chinking against the stones. I will stare through the water with dulling eyes at the mottled rot of leaves. Then I will just be a body in the river. But first we have to get there, wherever it is, wherever he chooses.

That's what you say, he says angrily, as though I'd lied to him about something important. *That's what you say.* Each time accentuating a different word with menace. If I could have figured out the nature of the crime, I'd have confessed to it. I haven't said a word since he let me out of the car.

I'm sorry, I answer. Anything else and he strikes me down. *That's what you say*, he says again. *I'm sorry*, I answer. Every step trying to save my life, every step trying to save my life. *That's what you say*, he says again. *I'm sorry*, I answer.

We come to a wide, waterless wash, an abandoned meander full of twisted willow wood. *Pee here*, he tells me. I pull down my shorts, my purple knit shorts with orange flowers, and I squat. *No, stand up and do it, damn it. You don't have to squat. You none of you have to squat.* This makes me cry, of all things this makes me cry, and I cry red in the face looking at him as I do it. Yes, I can pee like a mare with my legs wide apart, I can pee like a mare in a long hissing arc but I can't pee my initials to save myself, I can only make a trench in the sand. When I finish, he strikes me down. I see a red-tailed hawk. Lying on my back, a red-tailed hawk. I feel my skin burst dryly like burlap to a blade. His head blocks the sun. Big dark head, lumpen head like a charred walnut. I see the birds. Cottonwood seed floats like feathers, like angel down. The women are singing. The women bringing gingham and pie. The women who save me when he lumbers off through the underbrush and leaves me to bleed on dry sand.

That's a story that doesn't tell. It rewinds and it plays, but it doesn't tell. There's another that comes after.

That next spring Carson got his draft card, would soon have his diploma. *I know everyone has asked you lots of questions. Don't talk about it if you don't want to.* Was he begging me not to? The only question asked of me from the first and thereafter was *Are you all right?* What if I wasn't? What then? If I cried, would pity seal him to me? Anything I might have said was reminder of my defilement. Our loving was so untimely, I wish I could reset it like the hands of a clock.

The roadside fields were full of fireweed, Queen Anne's

lace, foxglove and tansy, a petit point of color beneath a tranquil sky. Goldfinches dipped their wings between the spiny violet disks of Bull Thistle blooms. Snowberries and elderberries tangled on the fences and further out in the field, where we went, islands of Nootka rose and blackberry bushes locked thorns and climbed each other. Rose hips gleamed a wet red.

He walked to the fence line and turned his back to me to relieve himself. When he bent his head to take himself out, I saw the tendons of his lean neck and the protective hunch of his shoulders. I was watching him as though I'd never see him again.

We crushed a place for ourselves in a profusion of oxeye daisies. With the soft flannel of his shirt against my face and the sun heating the crown of my head, I felt sleepy. I could forget we'd grown up. I'd used up days following Carson around with a tackle box and a can of worms in my hand. He fished, I read. We knew when to look at each other. But he was flushed with desire and anxiety. We had been waiting so long. We had been good and the bogey man had come anyway. Now Carson had to make the bogey man of nightmares go away. Of course we didn't say those things. We said other things. *If you don't want to . . . . I do want to, I do.* With all my heart, to this day still.

I studied his face, the inward turning tenderness of it, his lips always pooched out a little as though he were about to blow kisses. He pressed his lips against the pulse beneath my eyelid, stopped there, feeling it. After each touch, he stopped to register my response, my response registering in him. We knew each other well enough to enjoy our awkwardness. Pauses, small smiles, weight shifts, breath released with a satisfying sound. The total concentration of two on a blouse button as he worked it one-handed through. Tension, triumph, laughter. Then he pulled back a little to look at me. I had my hands around his forearms. I was trying to say *don't.* He pulled back and the features of his face flattened while the sun burst behind his head, his head a black blot against the sun. The moment of rigidity traveling down my spine inflicted a puncture; the desire seeped out of him all at once.

Maybe if I could have said why. Maybe if we could have been together in a well-lit room. He rolled away like a man taken by a bad wound. Then he lay on his back with his eyes closed. *I'm not strong enough,* he said after awhile, *I'm not strong enough.* I scratched at a thistle in my sock, noticed the erratic blooms of asters up and down the stalk. I was determined not to cry. My nipples chafed against the heavy starch of my blouse. He wasn't going to say more.

You've always been strong enough for me, you're strong enough now. But as I spoke my voice diminished, I realized it wasn't ourselves we were speaking of, our strength or desires, but the power of the event itself. My voice was diminished by the magnitude of the task I'd brought him to. Who could be strong enough to counter what had happened to me? I remembered seeing the small figurines Japanese women once carried to the doctor in their modesty, to point to what was the matter, and just as quickly slam the lid of the box shut. My body was an ivory figurine shut away in a box. I could point to what was the matter and Carson could try, but my whole body was the hurting thing. Carson kept his eyes shut, and for the first time I was afraid to touch him. It had never been an effort to be happy before. I saw a tear leak from one eye, trace its way down toward his temple. I leaned forward and put my lips to the tear, drinking it.

When basketball season started, Carson went with the women who would have him, one after another. It made him popular. There were terrible accusations and nasty rumors, but the way I saw it, he went off with whichever one fought hardest to claim him. I can't say there was any helping it. He couldn't look at me without seeing my hurt, his failure. Our pity for each other was so acute, it extinguished all desire.

My love for Carson is a weeping child I shut in a room at the end of the hall until the crying ceases. I am trying to teach my love a lesson, but long after, the sound quavers in my ears.

VIII.

This morning I decided I was actually going to call my father. I've been having breakfast with Donald Duck and Pluto Dog, two Disneyland mugs I turn to face me—same era as the Dinosaur Band-Aids. I found them at the back of the cupboard behind the cocoa. I've asked myself whether I keep using these things that belong to his children as a way to psych myself up or because I'm lonely and it really is comforting to look at their stupid faces. Anyway, I got up from the kitchen table, then suddenly I had to hold onto it. I thought I was going to go deaf or stop breathing. I heard this terrible noise, like a cave talking when the tide comes up, water sloshing in and air buffeting out and this low gurgle that gets louder . . . like I was trapped inside the giant's belly, rank air and briny water. To make it stop, I tried to quit breathing, forced my tongue to bulge up in the back of my throat till it hit my gag reflex and the Cheerios came back out, skewed upon the table in my own froth, looking like some unrescued shipwreck scene—tiny life preservers broken up, all heads bobbed under.

I pulled the T-shirt up off my belly and over my head, then I buried my face in it. Cotton softened by salt, it soothed me to smell home. I tried hard to think about the mother I'm mad at, not the one who would bring me ginger ale and saltines.

I dial his medical office and wait for the nurse to come on the line. She wants me to describe symptoms; she wants to have him call me back, but I can't leave him his own number. "I'll hold," I say, "however long."

There's a fake duck decoy on the coffee table. I flip its tail feather compartment open and shut. It's full of my father's golf tees. What is it I want to know from this man? For a moment, I feel like I can't remember. The story of my ancestors? How he could have thought it wouldn't matter to me to know who my people are? What difference will it make when I do know?

"Hello?" he comes on the line, an earnest tenor.

"Hello," I say after a moment.

"I hear you're feeling a little punk."

"I couldn't breathe for awhile, then I didn't want to, then I got sick."

My voice sounds like a cross-cut saw wrenched one direction then another.

"Sick in what way?"

"I threw up."

He asks me a whole series of questions. Have I had morning sickness? A fever? Any bleeding? Is there some-one with me? What I hear is the timbre of his voice, like a Bach cello suite playing on my mother's phonograph. His concern reduces me. *Oh Daddy, sob, I'm a do-over. I've lost my age. I can't count money. I can't ride a bus. Come and get me.*

"Don't be alarmed. The internal organs have less and less space as the baby gets bigger. There's a lot of pressure on the diaphragm and that can cause shortness of breath, sometimes dizziness. When was your last pre-natal exam?"

"I haven't had one."

"You haven't had one?"

I take a bronze boat bell off the table. It has no clapper so I hit it with my fingernail. It makes a tiny ping.

"Well, I went to a clinic to confirm the home pregnancy test, but I don't think that counts."

"Not if you didn't have an exam. How long since your last period?"

"Four months."

"So you're five months along and haven't seen a doc-tor?" He teeters on condemning, lurches away from it. "Can you tell me why? You don't have to of course."

"I'm afraid. I don't want anyone to look inside me, to let in the light. You know. The way you can't crack a door on a dark room or the pictures will all go black and you'll lose the faces."

"Well," he says, patiently, "I don't have to use a specu-lum. I don't have to open you to the light. But we should draw some blood for tests. You really must, for your baby's sake, get some medical attention."

Sob, sob, sob. Oh Daddy. "Oh thank you." *No speculum. Sob, sob, sob.*

"Honey," he says, "The hormones do get the better of women during pregnancy. Wild feelings aren't uncommon."

"I know. I know." *Wild feelings, wild feelings, wild feelings.*

"Promise me," he says, "that you'll come in this week."

I laugh abruptly. "Promise me you'll be there."

I hear a smile in his tone of voice. "Every day. I'm here every day."

Daddy'o, Daddy'o, promise me, please promise me, oh promise me . . .

Five minutes after I got off the phone, I found a bottle of antacids and swore at myself. What did I want him to be anyway? It was like hearing Mr. Roger's sing *You're Special to Me* and fantasizing that he was only broadcast to my house. Imagine how many women my father played the paternal role with everyday. Then I imagined his reaction if he knew how many men I'd slept with at the Getaway. And I meant something nice by it every time. I did.

IX.

Yesterday, I was taking inventory of the supply closets and I overheard a conversation between the three young men I'd hired to waterseal the cottage decks. At first I was amused, young men as helpless to their testosterone-pumped bodies as pregnant women are to the estrogen surges. And really the behavior is so similar—eating binges, mood swings, irascibility, grogginess. I was tallying up stacks of Sweetheart soap packages and Kleenex boxes and listening.

"So what happened over the weekend?"

"Nothing."

"Don't give me that."

"I'm telling you, nothing. The woman has no lips. I couldn't find anything to get a purchase on."

"You should go out with Sheila. Talk about lips. She could swallow a Frosty Snowcone."

"Is that a personal recommendation?"

"Maybe."

"Man, I don't want to get wet where you've been."

Then the conversation turned on Lyle, the youngest of them, not yet eighteen. I hadn't known he was an expectant father. But why should I? I don't hang around the P.O. boxes with the townies. He was quiet while the others enjoyed themselves at his expense.

"Any day now, huh, Lyle?"

"Yep, she's a week overdue."

"Boy, the tit fairy sure waved the wand on her."

"Jugs, man, milk jugs."

"I remember when my cat leaked milk all over our house."

"Gross out."

"What flavor do you think it'll be, Lyle? Chocolate, strawberry, vanilla."

"Hey Lyle, the demands are never gonna end now. Fu-fu needs a golden rattle and a silver spoon."

"How much are you gonna make an hour after you get your wages garnished? Think about that man."

"Look at the bright side. Maybe it'll be born mentally retarded and then the state will have to take care of it."

They all stopped in their tracks when I came around the corner shouting. "I heard that! Every word."

Randy and Chris exchanged glances, prepared to endure me and get it over with, but Lyle met my eye. I was shouting after all.

"I heard that! You little shits! On TV it may look like men run the world but this is my motel and I'm the reason your sorry asses have employment, except that you, Randy and Chris, no longer do. That's right. Get out of here."

Randy dropped his brush in the gallon of sealant and I watched while it sank. Chris said, "Shoee, Ms. Political," as he stepped off the deck of number 8. "Bet she never gets any."

"Shut up," said Randy as they headed for the truck.

I was so mad my scalp was sweating, and my eyes were stinging with tears. Then Lyle said quietly "Mrs. Friberg, you're going to have memorial tennis shoes on this patio if you don't move soon."

I was standing right in the damn sealant, the cheap rubber of my Payless sneakers on the verge of meltdown adhesion. I started laughing. "Aren't I a woman who won't budge?"

"Set in your ways, as they say," he ventured and smiled. Then he stepped off the patio and walked over the crab grass to my side and gave me a hand. *Scritch, scritch,* and I was free, standing close enough to him for a moment to see the cuts he'd made shaving. He stepped back respectfully and was silent, watching the blinker lights on the truck as it pulled out of the driveway. Then he spoke, his head slightly to one side, as though I might not want to look at him. "I was tired of those two jawing all day about what they could do to women. Thank you ma'am. I need this job."

I nodded, "You're welcome, Lyle. I'll keep you on as long as I can." Then I *squitched* my way to the office in as dignified a manner as I could manage. I sat on the steps unlacing my shoes, the image of the small lacerations on the underside of Lyle's neck so sweet and painful I wanted to run to him and tell him about Jess and the baby, but I didn't.

And why not? A soda, some solace, a break. With the right timing it amounts to a lot. I didn't used to think so. It was the kind of thing Jess would have done.

At The Albatross, there's a sign taped to the cash register: NO BRAINS, NO SERVICE. The massive back bar was brought down from a hotel in Alaska; black walnut cherubim frolic around the mirror, little rumps of innocence in love with temple columns and falling blossoms. It could make you maudlin except the place is so loud, there's no way to fall into a romantic reverie. Pool balls clack and roll on the table, the bartender dumps a lug of ice and swears, a man shouts over my head. The sounds keep me nervous, shaken up like salad dressing.

I know the bartender, Maynard. He's a tile and mortar man, did a bang-up job on a bathroom when the black and pink tile floor buckled. He's got snappy blue eyes, and he's never let anyone bother me. His reputation for having a temper is local lore—supposedly he left a spade in some guy's head years back yelling "Want a piece of pie?" Now he's so swollen with booze and bellicosity, his red cheeks look like they've been pattied up for the grill.

"How're you?" I ask.

"F.I.N.E." he answers, spelling it out. "Fucked-up, Insecure, Neurotic, and Emotional. How about you?"

I shrug. "My daughter's helping me build character, I'm developing a Mt. Rushmore brow. Can you see the scaffolding on my forehead, the little guys pinging away with ball-peen hammers."

He squints at me smiling. "Right, another goddamn growth experience."

"She's putting me through changes." I banter, because he knows I'm not here for specifics. *Just the red red robin bob bob bobbin along.*

After he's fixed my brandy, Maynard suddenly reaches across the bar and lands a handshake next to my shoulder. "Frank, how's it going?" From my perspective, the handshake looks like a moment of miniature thumb wrestling. When it's over I look down the length of arm anchored to

man-bulk, this *basso profundo* standing behind me and stirring up the hair on my neck.

"Me?" Frank fairly shouts, "I'm putting 30,000 dollar
nets in the water and bringing up nothing. I own the boat
and I haven't made a crew share. I'd sell my house but my
ex-wife is in it. The bank's about to repossess my boat.
That's this season."

"Drink coming up," Maynard says, making a long
amber pour into a barrel glass.

"Hey, get her one too," he motions towards me. "I bet
you like a man who doesn't try to impress you with money."

I flicker over him, quick take on the man: an impression
of glistening, darkly, green eyes, a moment of engagement.
So what of it? What's it to you? He juts his jaw at me, looks
back to Maynard. Then I try not to look, but I feel the man's
weight shifting onto the bar stool. I can hear the creasing
and uncreasing of his leather jacket as he gets his wallet out.
I keep my vision peripheral, limited to the black jacket
which is so old the wear marks show the brown of the original hide, beyond that the belt and the Buck knife sheath and
the swell of one buttock.

"Hey," he says to me, more directly. "You look like a
garden party and I look like I'm going to a rumble. Mind if
I pull up?"

"No," I say, shrugging habitually. "I like a man who
doesn't try to impress me."

"Because no man can, right?" He laughs easily. I've
seen him around for years.

"It's boring to be a trained seal with a ball on your
nose," I answer. More ice crashes behind the bar and suddenly nothing is funny to me anymore. If I told these guys
about my workmen, wouldn't they shrug it off as some foolishness? Bar humor. The down-and-out, the underdog, the
disillusioned, the dead-end, the fears self-fulfilled, and my
downy cheeked child forced to chug-a-lug her first fill of it.
I turn fully towards him, in case that's what he wants: a
look.

"Listen, I don't have to laugh at your bitter jokes."

"Hey, I only laugh at my own jokes out of courtesy. I
was raised to be polite." He puts one elbow on the bar,

effectively shielding himself from me and lights a cigarette.

I sigh in a long stream of smoke. "I'm sorry. I don't like men much in general."

He turns back to look at me. My age is enough to let him know I'm not trying to be cute and challenging; I don't try to gauge my looks much anymore. I'm a weather vane, still recognizable. His dark eyes are set too close together, his rather large nose actually has a divot in it, he's got vertical wind lines on both cheeks and a jaw like an icebreaker's prow—a face made for flinching.

"I'm one in a multitude, darling," he says, up-ending his drink until the ice cubes crash against his teeth, down-ending it with precision. "And I'm not going to try to *im*press you or *de*press you or *com*press you or even *press* you. I don't like pressure myself."

"Were you in Vietnam?"

"Bingo. But you won't find me shouting about buddies and bodies in your ear. I don't like to talk about it."

"So what do you shout about?"

He raises an eyebrow skeptically and smiles. Clearly, the subject is off limits. Then he goes on. "Let's talk about this. When a lady looks at you like she's got to be afraid. And some son of a bitch has given her good cause. Most you can do is look at her before the light changes to green and gun it."

"It's true. Anything you say only makes you more suspect."

"So all that's left is how you look when you're saying it. No impression you can make, only one she can take."

He snorts and looks at me then back at the bar mirror. When he shouts, I twitch.

"Hey, Maynard, Gallon up. Bring the lady a refresher." The bartender spins back from the bottles and gives me a bemused, flattering look. Frank turns back to me; he's on a roll.

"What's the smartest thing I can think of? Don't analyze other people's pain. Don't assume it's going to make sense." His nostrils flare and his eyes are stark and wide. "One guy was my neighbor, lost part of his head in 'Nam. They filled it up with putty or something, covered it over.

When we got back, he used to go to this one spot and just watch the water, you know, for hours. Then this business man comes along and builds a big old house. One day, they find the whole family dead, knifed. That's why he did it . . . cause the guy blocked his fucking view. What does that tell you about war?"

"Maybe he should have just put the guy's eyes out."

He taps his finger to his lips, looking at me a moment.

"When I came back, I used to touch up old photos, an uncle's business. Once I'm touching up a photo for a family whose son had died. In the picture, his eyes were closed. They wanted me to paint them open. Shit, it creeped me, like prying back the corpse's lids, dreaming about some really terrible accusatory look. And the whole family fighting over what color this kid's eyes were."

It's a good story. His voice rumbles out a rhythm and my body responds to the bass line in his voice . . . must be why I feel like fighting with him.

"Eye color's important enough in a family to fight about."

"I know, I know," he says, waving his ash over the bar. "Except I couldn't determine it for these people. Here." He's riffling through his wallet, unstuffing it all over the bar. "Here," he hands me a tiny portrait of a madonna and child, "that's whose eyes I painted, icon eyes, like all the ones I could remember watching me, watching my back go out that door." He extinguishes his cigarette by rolling the ember off the end and leaving it to die out, and he won't look at me, determined to watch the last wisps as some ritual of wretchedness.

I snort some of my smoke at him. "Yeah, well, I lost someone to 'Nam, his face is blurry now, all of him really, except his hands." *I remember his hands as if no one else had ever touched me.*

He turns his eyes to me, a charismatic flicker far off in the darkness, a flame I begin to walk towards across primordial cess. Then we extinguish it by looking back into our drinks.

"So," he says, looking up abruptly and lighting another cigarette.

"Where's your old man, old rain in the face?"

"I keep him in a test tube."

"Nah," he answers, "You're not into that cryogenics and sci-fi dry ice. Bring him back when he's grateful, right?"

"No, I don't want him back at all. I mean it. I had a daughter by artificial insemination."

He stubs out his cigarette with a lot of unnecessary mashing and says "Yeah but . . ." then turns to me abruptly. "It belonged to this dead guy right, the one you loved in 'Nam."

"No, but I wished it did, sometimes I almost believed it."

"I get it," he says, nodding not to me but the bar, "I got your number. I dialed it."

"Talking about the war. Isn't this like carbon dating bones or counting tree rings? Seeing how far back the marks go."

"I don't care how we do it. Carbon date me if you have to. Count the rings around my eyes. But date me. We'll take a drive, okay?" I look at him long enough to acknowledge the question, then straight ahead. I want to see the side of his face that isn't turned toward me, that's reflected in the backbar mirror, but he's onto me, looking already at us there, as though we were in another room, split-off dream doubles whose intensity and urgency is everywhere apparent. In the mirror, I can't resist it; his face is openly waiting and hurting and blameless.

"Those people," he says, making a hook of his thumb and gesturing toward the mirror, "They want to talk to us." But by now I'm rummaging around for more cigarettes, hunting for something ironic to say, but feeling leached of it —the urge toward irony the only bit of residue left.

"Here," he says, expertly sliding his pack on the bar so that two are exposed. "Have one of mine."

But in my mind we're still moving around in the mirror-room like sleepwalkers. I imagine Heaven Hotel—a suite in the sky, silver outside our windows, a room that begins with the small pleasures of anticipating pleasure.

"Listen," I say, "I came here to make myself cry. My daughter ran away. I never normally come here. I usually drink at home."

"And I'm messing up your plans by making you laugh?" He alternates beats with the thumb and finger of one hand against the wood. "What? You want to be alone? You want to read the paper? Here, I'll get it for you, that'll cheer you up."

He actually gets up off the stool before I grab his arm, but I've got my purse hooked to my wrist and I'm trying to save my drink. There's too much of the man and he takes me with him. I fall to my knees before he scoops me up by my armpits and deposits me back on my stool. He stays there, heating the air close to my face, and I feel like a child who has been lifted up high and set on a counter to see everything—restful when the fluster passes. He still has his arm up my back, steadying and solid as the back of a chair. "Schucks," he says, "You didn't have to propose. I'm too old for that shit anyway."

I let myself laugh. I let my forehead fall onto his chest with a satisfying thunk. Nice knowing he wouldn't mind if I beat it against him for awhile. Finally I look up at him. "So you've been married?"

"Plenty," he says. "I'm Portuguese" (he pronounces it Portugezay). "You know, put the net right in. Bring up the house payment, bring up the phone bill. Send a card: Wishing you were her. Oops. Onto my future ex-wife. I should have shot myself but it's against my religion."

"What about with your kids."

"Solid," he says fiercely, "Whatever they need. Like an automatic money machine. Ka-ching, ka-ching, ka-ching. Resupply. How it should be. I love'em. Here, let's drink to our kids. We'll cry about your daughter later." We raise our glasses "Gallon up, baby," he says. "Let's buff and duff."

.

The parking lot smells of slough and slutch—fertility at low tide in the marsh mud. Frank drives a Cutlass Cruiser station wagon and to look at its fake wood sides I *know* she got the house, he got the car. But he's modified it with a bumper sticker that reads, *Jesus was a gillnetter,* and long tool boxes in the back. We drive north a few miles where Loomis Creek broadens to the sea. It's close to nine o'clock and the sun is setting. Our faces inside the car appear black and white against the vast pink sky. I see only the sculptural lines of his face—the way twenty years ago he would have been handsome.

I tell him how the topography on this bend of road always makes me feel like a traveler instead of someone who lives a few miles beyond. The creek runs south alongside the sea before it turns west to open its mouth. The sun setting on the ocean reflects in the creek's currents. Reflections doubling. No wonder my heart anticipates something unnamed. I'm looking for an opening, the way the creek must look for an opening to the sea. Frank pulls over on a rise and kisses me. It's very slow and deliberate and almost comical the way he slides his girth out from behind the wheel and his leather coat arms uncrease loudly, and all the while I'm watching—comical because there's a hint of parody for us both, because we did this seriously a million years ago when we were lithe and sweaty. His kiss is sweet, tentative, sucky, we take little peeks at each other before our tongues foray further. At last, having gone for the gullet in juvenile fashion, we stop to laugh, let the parody catch up with us. When he smiles he looks goofy, the way clowns do—by sustaining sincerity. I fight my mind's sarcastic asides and I don't look away when he holds my face in his hands. I feel shy suddenly, shyer than I could possibly have known about myself.

"I need to get home now."

"Why? You afraid you're going to use up all the good time and have a shortage later?"

"I'm afraid if I have a good time, I'll know how bad it's been."

On the way home, I tell him about Jess. He nods a lot and we smoke.

"It's true," he says, "You've never known worry tll you've had kids."

We pull into my motel and I try the door handle on my side. It's frozen. He's already out and piling around to my side. "I'm sorry, it's stuck."

I yell out the wind wing. "I love it. Car comes with a doorman."

My cottage smells like old cantaloupe rinds from break-fast simmering with cigarette butts under the kitchen sink.

"Gad" I say, going for the trash.

"Here," he says, swinging the can away from me by its rim. "Round back, right?"

While he's doing that, I go into the bathroom to brush my teeth and wash my face. I'm relieved that he acts his age, that he doesn't mind taking the trash out first. I simply can't imagine persevering in the performance of passion while foremost is the need to pee. It was never worth it. I come out and turn sideways in the hall as he passes me. "My turn to buff and duff," he says, going by me and shutting the door.

Just before I switch off the standing lamp, I see Jess's picture on the mantle, her senior year in high school when she refused to smile. I'm waiting for her to come home and tell me to take it down. Tell me she can't stand it anymore. I can't stand it anymore. Frank's coming down the hall. Daughter, would this make you smile?

In the dark, I'm dismayed, afraid it's going to be the old penis polka, worrying about whether his erection is up or down, hard or soft, just as self-conscious as stepping all over each other's feet wishing the tempo weren't so mad-dening. And I can't help it, the thing itself, the impression it leaves on my belly is the stamp of an old memory.

"Hey, girl," he says, his thumbs at my temples stroking lightly.

"I'm not good at this, Frank," I say, shaking my head, "not good. I was never good."

"Okay, okay, okay," he says. "Let's just pretend we're plants."

"What?"

"Yeah, you're the wild rose grew round the briar. Or maybe I'm the wild rose grew round the briar. "

"You're lulu," I say, laughing.

"No, I'm a plant. We hardly move. An inch a decade."

Then we don't talk. His kisses are like little plush blooms. After awhile, an unrolling, a darting out, a little tendril that takes root. For now, kissing is so much better than making love—none of the banal awkwardness of old

injuries and elbows in the wrong places and breasts slop-
ping to the side and getting pinched between your body and
his, or knee caps smacking together, or balls squished, all
that posturing and positioning. Bodies and faces the way
Braque would paint them, full of fissures, disjointed features, angular, broken up, a cheese grater for teeth, a man-
dolin for an ear. I've always wanted to suspend the kiss.

Frank made the transition from his imagination to my
arms so gracefully. The all-night kiss, face between my
legs, hands clasped over my belly, he looks up like he's
praying, supplicant who will not rise off his knees until
finally I've slid down to him, spent, panting, crouched
inside his rounded torso, outlined by the light so that black-
ness pools between the nobs of our bones.

He clears his throat softly. "I wish I could have . . ."

"Sshh."

"You don't mind that I . . ."

"Sshh. I wanted it to be like this."

In the morning he tells me a joke. "What's the difference between twenty years of the same job and twenty years
of marriage?" I stare at him groggily on my way to the bathroom. "The job still sucks." I laugh as I go down the hall but
his insecurity is beginning to wear on me and I notice things
I'd rather not, like the guinea pig whorl at the crown of his
head because he hasn't combed his hair yet and the fact that
he's having a cigarette on an empty stomach. Well, he made
his own coffee, that's something.

"You don't run out of jokes, do you?" I say.

"Not all day," he says, leaning back in his chair so I can
see him, so he can holler down the hall. "Not if I can help
it."

But at the breakfast table he keeps the verbal percussion
down until I can get some coffee, and I wonder what
unlovely characteristics of mine he's noticing by the morn's
early light.

"So fishing is a pretty unpredictable life, isn't it?" I push
down the toaster button and don't say what's on my mind.
How futile any feeling would seem if last night were just a
one night stand. And yet I already want him to go away. I'm

itching with it. For me, nothing can last and yet I want to believe it will. It's a terrible strain to live inside the paradox: always being prepared to leave and needing to believe I won't have to. I'd just as soon boil an egg alone and I know it.

Frank shrugs. His eyes are looking inward as he speaks, not at me.

"Fishing is a life of worrying when the fish aren't there, planning and laying odds on the next week, changing your mind about leaving or staying, staying or leaving, worrying about losing more money if you stay or being absent when the fish hit. You're damned if you do and damned if you don't and when you rake in the cash, the guys think you're a shrewd motherfucker and you think you're just plain lucky."

"Are you a shrewd motherfucker?" He's at the table and I'm leaning on the counter. My tone is tougher than I had intended. It makes us both aware that I haven't crossed the linoleum to join him again.

He stirs his coffee slowly, his stare an assessment also. "Are you going to see me again?" he asks.

"I don't know. We're still on best behavior. I don't like it when that wears off." What I really want is for him to convince me he'll never hurt me, to shoulder the weight of my whole history, but I feel angry that my desires are so corny and impossible, and even to my own ears I simply sound spiteful.

"So, this is modern romance as in 'Farewell, I liked you?'" He's tapping his finger to his lips, and it stings me that already I recognize the meaning of his gestures. How far will I take it?

"Romance, Frank? Or merely pathos." My bitchiness feels so satisfying, like making a clean tear in an old sheet. I can't seem to help myself.

He gulps down the rest of his coffee standing up and makes an exaggerated Ahhh sound. "Ciao, Bella," he says, as he puts the cup down. His eyes are bright with fury.

I watch his feet make dust devils down my driveway while my daughter stares at me stonily from her high school picture, as though she expected this from me, as though she couldn't be more disgusted. Before I know it, I'm running out the door in my plaid flannel nightshirt yelling, conscious even as I do so of a million stupid movie scenes and my absurd willingness to star in this one. But when I get to the car, I don't know what to say. He hasn't started the engine yet; he's smoking a cigarette and leaning against the door. Waiting. Evidently he doesn't know how to be in the movies.

"So what is it?" he says, hunching his shoulders, "I forget my lunch?"

"No," I say, "This isn't how it's supposed to be."

"What is? darlin." He looks at me and shakes his head.

"I want you to come inside, and don't believe me again if I ask you to leave."

He lets me stand there for a long moment—disheveled, bare feet on the gravel— then he reaches out and tugs on my sleeve. I take the two strides between us and he collars me affectionately though I keep staring at the ground. "This could be a bad habit, sweetheart, asking me to get lost. Do you think you could break yourself of it?"

"I could try."

X.

News comes to my kitchen door. I hear the screen rattle as he knocks lightly on the door frame. It's Nigel wearing a raw silk shirt of cobalt blue that brings out the color in his eyes. He has dressed to be handsome today. Surely not for me, the old lesbo mother.

"Jess isn't here," I call out.

"May I come in anyway?"

I let him be uncomfortable for a moment as I stub out my cigarette, then I make an open-palmed gesture with my hand, acquiescing rather than welcoming. I don't want to consign him to being the bastard yet, not if he's felt an opening in himself and come here to widen it.

"Will she be back soon?" He holds his hand against the screen door so it won't slam as he comes inside.

"I doubt it. She's six states away. Gone to visit relatives in the Midwest."

Ah," he says gracefully, neither putting me on the spot nor revealing what he might know. I have an urge to bring him up short.

"Her father's family. Won't you sit down?" He takes a seat at the breakfast table, looking at the old fashioned silver toast holder I've got stuffed with mail and my coffee-splotched, jam-splattered table cloth; he keeps his face carefully composed.

"That must have been hard on you both, losing him when Jess was so young."

The pause that follows is altogether too long for a woman whose husband has been dead twenty years. Of course I'm not that woman. His eyes flicker as he openly studies me. I can presume now that he knows about the insemination but is he dispensing kindness or trying to cut a deal of sorts? He will defer to me in this if I defer to him in other matters? My voice is caustic.

"Isn't consolation for the widow a bit overdue?"

"We've never really had a conversation."

I carry the ashtray to the table and sit across from him. "What do you want to talk about?"

He laughs but it's a manufactured sort of chuckle, on the defensive.

"Well, maybe there are things we should talk about . . . arrangements."

He clears his throat and looks at me levelly, as if to remind me that we're peers, closer in age certainly than he and Jess. "I'm perfectly willing to pay child support. If we can't agree on a figure then whatever sum the state sets, given my income."

"That's decent of you." I say this genuinely, knowing she'd resent the immediacy with which I boil down to practicalities. It's not for me to say more. I don't know what Jess wants. I told her that if she wanted to be done with him, we'd manage, but I'd like to see her finish the degree at the community college, at least.

"Of course, that's after the DNA tests determine that it's mine."

I sit back from the table and scratch at the flower pollen that has made mustard colored explosions on the cloth. The daisies droop in their vase and the water smells of ferment. Ten days ago, Jess picked them. Nigel reaches into his jacket pocket and takes out his own cigarettes. His hands are elegant: long fingers and flexible, slender thumbs that bend back as he gestures. I imagine their skill on her body.

"Do you have reason to think otherwise?" I ask.

"Possibly, but I'd rather not discuss it." He says this with one eye shut against a match flame and a cigarette pressed between his lips.

"Too bad it doesn't happen in your body. Or you'd be suspect. Man over forty, unmarried."

"What about yourself?" he says, laughing uneasily.

"Exactly," I say. "In this community, I'm considered capable of anything."

"You look like you might be."

His charm is evident to me. The invitation to spar, to show myself a little. How winning it is for a man to openly admire a woman for her contrary, antagonistic nature. But this isn't a subject for intellectual flirtation.

I respond sternly: "For the sake of this conversation, let's give her the benefit of the doubt."

He watches the tiny sulfur fumes that escape from his match in the ashtray, gauging the edge in my voice. "Look," he says, weary in his distinctly cosmopolitan fashion, "All of a sudden she's trying to make us into some major love story because she's pregnant. I was honest with her from the beginning."

But not with yourself, I think. All these tired phrases, tired as the people who utter them, believing love and only love will change them, with the right person they can be good. Shift of responsibility. I'm glad he's not foolish enough to believe the baby will be the right person. Maybe we're all lucky for that.

"So you told her you didn't want to get involved. You're too old, too incorrigible, too dented from the last go round. Right? So tell me, how do you make love without being involved?"

"Well, you are involved, but as a friend. She accepted that. She knew I couldn't be in love with her."

What he says sounds like recitation, as though he's said it many times before but is ashamed in front of me to infuse it with the necessary authority. He says it to the stinking daisies.

I scoff. "You're the older man here. You know better than to believe that. The heart always wants more. Her love would heal you. She's too young to be jaded." And I think to myself, you wouldn't have been attracted to her if she were as callous as you are.

"She's more mature than you think."

I think . . . . I think she hid what was youngest in her. The girl who sat at this table last week let me make her sandwiches and pour her milk. Oh, I know what he might say. A mother's love debilitates the almost grown. But lovers let each other be little. Succor and solace. She doesn't know that yet. I see his hardened air of self-preservation though I don't know its causes.

"More mature than I think, but too young to know what she's doing? How can she be both?"

"Easy, mature about some things but not about others. C'mon, you're a mother."

"Her mother. And I trust her judgement. Maturity doesn't mean she has to come to my conclusions."

"Well, I'm too old for her anyway. I was just trying to be a mentor of sorts."

He has a sudden need to press the bridge of his nose. "Of sorts," I echo. "Now you're reversing the equation. You're not right for her. Too old. You're doing us all a favor. You fail to win my empathy, though it may be there's nothing you can do about that."

I want to tell him that lovers don't believe in reasons and some have succeeded because of it. But I feel so invalid on the subject.

"I told her I was too old for her, that she ought to move on. I tried to make it easy for her to leave."

"But you didn't leave."

He shrugs, looking past the kitchen wall to something far off, his own life maybe. "I get lonely. I'm human."

"You're human," I say, nodding. "That much I'll concede. I'm going to make coffee."

As I scoop coffee from the cannister, I feel suddenly what a relief it is to turn my back on him. My God, I'm good at it, but I'm trying not to make the same recommendation for Jess. The coffee maker gurgles like a swimmer going down and I look at Nigel who is staring out my window, evidently as relieved as I am. It's an ugly reflection, the two of us alike in this way. He would banish the baby; I would banish the father. *You're human all right, Nigel, but you don't know much about it yet.* He's one of these men with fancy dare devil hobbies like flying gliders in Nevada, deep sea diving in the Maldives or Azores. He keeps risking his life to try and know something about it, to feel it taken and given back in the same moment. Jess will know more than the moment, but he doesn't think of that. Only if he went through labor with her, would he know. And suddenly I am remembering the first sensations of pregnancy, the blastocyst burrowing in, the cramps that feel like sand crabs scuttling, widely dispersed diggings that occur all of a sudden, vanish, reoccur elsewhere.

"When did you see her last?" I ask, turning and leaning against the counter.

"A month ago. She said she hoped we could be friends. I told her I didn't think so. I remember now those little comments she made early on about not feeling well. She thought she had the flu. Bullshit. She said her periods were irregular. I don't buy it. She didn't have to miss a second period."

"Deception is never admirable, but if she didn't intend to abort, what difference does it make now? More time to argue? Surely, in all your wisdom, you can see that."

"She's had an abortion before," he says, lighting another cigarette, looking at me carefully to see if he's shocked me again. He hasn't.

"You think that makes it easier? It doesn't." I'm shouting now. I want to turn on him, but all I have in my hands is the dishtowel. I feel hard against them both now, the same way Jess has felt toward her father and me at times no doubt. "It makes me understand even less about what she was doing with you. You'd think at least a woman would change after an abortion, quit dating men who can't even talk about children. I told her that in high school. Perhaps you just seemed a safe bet, a *fatherly* age."

I'm practically sneering at him, a safe distance away at the butcher block. He jumps up from the table and I think he's going to storm out, but instead he holds himself rigidly in front of a wall covered with kitchen art as though now were the time to take in some paintings. The blue one Jessica painted years ago with her feet; I hope he can see the tiny prints. I remember her pounding against me from the inside. She always came alive in me when I was swimming, full term in the heat of summer. I spent the early evenings at Tenant Lake, when the crowds were down and before the mosquitos came out. Arms over my head for the big slow strokes. I could breathe easier and she had more room. My lugubrious body suddenly buoyant, in full motion and full of motion as she whirled and churned inside me. I was swimming with the baby swimming inside me. And as I floated in duck weed and turned slowly beneath a white and yellow sky, I felt myself too, swimming inside a creature swimming. It seems important to tell him this, but I can't think of how.

He turns toward me at last, then looks up at the ceiling as though something there were waiting to save him.

"I know what you're saying, but I'm not in love with her. Okay?"

"I bet you're in love each and every time." My voice is venomous and I'm afraid to pour him hot coffee. "She's perfect until you know her. Then the responsibility is all hers, for changing, ruining it for you."

"Maybe you're right, but who I am shouldn't be any surprise to her. I wasn't exactly 'the boyfriend.'"

"Everything is a surprise to her, believe me. How real the baby is, that he commands her course even this early. Sudden fatigue like a trap door. The need to lie down. She can't will her way anymore. And how much she loves the baby is a surprise to her. So why not you too? You could have surprised her."

"No, I can't." He sighs. His eyes are asking me not to hate him. "I didn't want her to have any false hope."

"Well, she didn't give you any false ideas either, did she? You blame her because she's the first to know and the last one who can do something about it. Did you expect me to recommend abortion? This is my grandchild!" I stop to draw breath. When I say the word child, we both hush, as though we had been caught fighting. I reach for coffee mugs. The cabinet door comes unstuck abruptly and all the cups within rattle. I feel the cool cupboard air along the undersides of my arms and wish for all the world I could climb in there.

"You take sugar?" I ask at last.

He comes across the room looking flushed like a boy, suddenly mindful of his manners, shadowing me as I pour. I try to open a bag of macaroons but I can't pluck the tough cellophane between my fingers because it's so tight. "Do you mind?" he takes it from me and tears it with his teeth in a flash of white. "There," and we both start stupidly arranging cookies on the plate. "I'm sorry," he says, "I shouldn't have come empty-handed." The words seem to reverberate on the air for a long time, but I don't rush in to stop it. We sit back down though neither of us wants coffee or cookies by now. I decide to satisfy my own curiosity in case it's my only chance.

"Was your own family so bad that you never want one?"

"No, no. It's nothing like that. I mean I probably look

ridiculous saying this, but I do want a family . . . eventually
. . . when I'm ready."

When I speak next, it's with Jessica's words and I shock
myself by sounding amused. "Nobody asks to be born. It's
the first thing inflicted on you. You're blaming her because
you feel like something is being *done to you* meantime she's
watching her body and wondering *why me?* You could be
kinder," I say.

He taps one finger on the table methodically and
watches it. When he looks up, I know he's about to make an
admission that will cost him. "I could be a lot of things."

We said goodbye not long after, with a peculiar sense of
collusion. He asked me to call him if I heard from her, and
to tell her that he wanted to talk. I asked him to call me if
he heard from her, and to let her know I wanted to talk. We
didn't shake hands, just backed away from each other. I'm
not used to sharing concern and neither is he. When he
walked away, he nearly wrung his neck on the clothesline
but at the last minute he saw it and shoved it upward with
one hand.

XI.

The young nurse at my father's office has an adenoidal voice and she wears a flower barrette made out of popsicle sticks. All the way down the hall, she talks over her shoulder but not to me. She makes quips to the other staff in their little side rooms with counters, and they all laugh jovially at some running joke. I catch a glimpse of my father, his profile as he stands at a counter talking into a hand-held recorder. His hair has silvered at the sides but in back it gleams like copper. "Ah, gosh," the nurse says to me in the room, blowing her bangs off her forehead and wrapping the blood pressure cuff on. By the time she listens to my heart, her face is serious. "You worried about something, honey?" Then she leaves me with pages of questionnaire to fill in. *Family history of congenital defects such as cleft palate or club foot; mental illness such as schizophrenia or manic depression; other as in hypertension, diabetes, rheumatoid arthritis; cardiovascular diseases as in strokes, or heart attacks; chromosome abnormalities as in Down's syndrome; genetic diseases as in cystic fibrosis, hemophilia.*

I fill in what I can, then write cryptically *reason I am here.* Such a range of mortality, oddly it affirms me even as it frightens me. There are reasons I need to tether myself at this end of the lifeline. I look for something in the room to tell me more about my father. The black vinyl stool, the utility sink, pump soap, boxes of white latex gloves, tray with swabs and speculum: all standard. The walls are greenish beige covered in overstylized water-color health department posters: your circulatory system, your nervous system, your respiratory system, your internal organs. Each poster shows the same man leaping for a volleyball: Mr. Circulatory, Mr. Respiratory, Mr. Nervous, Mr. Intestine. I don't mind the cross section views where the man and woman look like their front halves fell off exposing male and female reproductive systems, but it's getting to be close quarters with the peeled clone men.

I almost want to put on the gown, let my father examine me so I can feel his hands upon me, as though there might be some similarity between how he would have touched me as a baby and how he would touch me now as a stranger. Doctor's hands have to be protective, deliberate, gentle. Yet he chose to be a doctor so those qualities are also simply the man and not the professional. I'm afraid I will close my eyes if I let him touch me and make a sound in my throat. My head rolls back at the thought and something catches my eye. Pictures on the ceiling, above the examining table. Birds—crimson cardinals and yellow finches, bright flittings across a swallowing green—somewhere to look when you lie there. A way for your mind to take flight. So he thinks of these things . . . .

The door opens and in he comes. His eyes are green-brown with yellow behind them, the color of an algae bloom backlit by the sun. Like my own. Introductions over with, the official ones anyway, he leans back on his heels and reads my chart. I wish his pallor were less pasty but I'm glad to see he's still lean, wiry even—he'll grow old stooped and stiff of gait but out walking, bird watching maybe. "Okay," he says, with a dip in his voice, to alert me. I wish I could float in a small bubble behind his head for the day, simply observe him, see where our mannerisms and movements match. There's no explaining my pleasure in this. Evidently, he's asked me a question and I've completely missed it. He sets down the chart and squints at me for a moment but doesn't repeat it.

"Are you sure you haven't been in before? Maybe when you were a child?"

"Not that I know of."

"Well, you look familiar anyway," he says jocularly, as he turns on the faucets over the sink.

"I should."

It's odd the way anger rises in me when he addresses me directly. I don't want him to alter this moment of discovery where he is all mine and doesn't know it. If I could, I would shrink him in a children's story and keep him in a glass box.

"You what?" A wry, little smile creeps to his lips. He's going to play it cool, but he's perked up with interest. Apparently, he likes oddity.

"I should look familiar even though you've never met

me." I can't help it. I want this moment to extend, to lengthen and slow the way people who have been in accidents describe it. The thrill is quite close to total panic.

"Why's that?" He's tosses the towel he's dried his hands on and crosses his arms.

"I'm your daughter by artificial insemination. I found you in the yearbook. Class of '69. You're my father."

His eyes are wild for a moment, like a horse's rearing, and he holds the countertop he's leaning against. Then he focuses hard on me.

"What makes you so sure it's me?"

"Do you have a mirror we can stand in front of?" I pick up a lock of my hair. "Or shall I get out the picture of you when you were almost my age."

He takes a long, deep breath. "I may be your biological father, yes, but the man who raised you is your real father."

"What if I told you he was some asshole macho who never got over having defective sperm, always intimidated his kid to prove he was a real man, treated me like the product of an affair? What if I was never able to love him and wished to hell he wasn't my father and felt guilty. And nobody ever told me."

"People can feel that way about their biological fathers anyway. The one you want to rail at is him not me."

"My mother raised me alone, but don't worry, I'm used to not having a father by now. I didn't come here to acquire a parent."

"Good," he said, "Because you won't." His look assessed me for some toughness he found and of which he was approving. I couldn't believe I was being so predictably adolescent. Because I only had this once? I had to know him now, sting him and be stung? Determine his patience, his tolerance, his threshold in three minutes?

He walked to the shiny metal cabinet and looked at himself, his reflection in the dulled matt of scratched metal, a face entirely stilled. He laughed brusquely after a moment, as if to throw a stone into the stillness, saying, "I always wanted to know how I would look, receiving the kind of news I deal out."

"I'm not a disease, you know."

"No, you're not. And not all the news I deliver is unhappy tidings either." He looked at me kindly then, with great curiosity. I smiled to see it. Our brief flash of anger had refreshed us both—fear purged. "You were afraid I would regard you as some achievement of my own, suddenly unveiled with the wisk of a sheet."

"Yes, that would have been the worst, worse than not finding you."

"What drove you to it?"

"She didn't tell me there was a semen donor. Someone else told me last year." It wasn't what I wanted to say. The end of secrecy had driven me to it. Secrecy was the one thing he and my mother had agreed to even though they had never met.

"Who told you?"

"My mother's ex-lover. After she moved out. Maybe she thought I had a right to know, maybe she was just pissed off. But there I was, all the stories I built myself from suddenly untrue. My mother had told me I was the daughter of her first love, a guy who got killed in Vietnam, and she had all these other tragic stories to go with it."

"But you can understand why she wanted you to believe that."

I started to laugh, but it came back at me fast in that little white and metal room. It had sounded so odd to hear him speak of her, counseling me as though he knew her. For a moment I felt that I could just put them on the phone together and then go on home.

"Christ! Of course I can understand. But isn't anyone supposed to try to understand me?"

"I'm sorry. I can see why you laughed. I spoke with such familiarity."

Suddenly I felt the need to defend her. "It's not that she wasn't a good mom. She is. She owns and runs a motel. Before that, she was a school teacher. She's brave and tough and funny."

"Did she help you find me?"

"Yes, after our explosion."

"Well, that says a lot."

In the glare of his curiosity, I feel all my love for her

flood to the surface, like a massive opening of capillaries, roaring in my ears. I've waited all this time to find my father and suddenly I want to shove him aside and find a phone so I can at least call her. But he's talking again.

"I understand now why you didn't put the gown on. I'll get one of my partners to examine you, if you like."

It's clear to me now how it might look to her . . . how easy for me to come in here for fifteen minutes and like him . . . how easy for me to live with her all my life and be mad . . . . I resist him with a new fount of rage.

"Can you imagine if you had examined me? Can you imagine if we slept together? I've slept with men as old as you and I've wondered if I might sleep with one of my brothers by mistake. You know, there's no central registry in this country."

"Yes, I know that. Still, it's a remote possibility."

"Statistically speaking, yes. But you've never felt what it's like to wonder about it. How would you like it if I wanted to meet my brothers, the three boys you have."

"They're old enough that I think they could handle it . . . if you wanted to make the trip. One's in California, one's in Detroit, and the other's in the Peace Corps in Namibia."

"How about your wife?"

He shrugged. "She already thinks the worst of me. We divorced years ago. My boys were four, six, and eight when we ended the marriage. Leaving my boys was the hardest thing I ever did. Last year, when Scott was about to start a family, he wanted me to talk about that time, and I realized that he needed to know that was the hardest thing I ever did. But I don't have a story like that for you."

"I know. You sired me instead of parented me."

He sighs, rests his elbows on his knees and stares at his hands. When he looks up his eyes are level with mine.

"Does it help to know that I wondered about you, just as you did about me."

"What kinds of things did you wonder?"

"I hoped, like any parent, that you would grow up relatively healthy and happy, undamaged by the million and one dangers of the world, that you would have a passion for something you could arrange your life around so that it would make sense to you."

"I'm just mad all the time. That seems to be my passion."

"Maybe social reform is your calling. It requires steady outrage." He smiles at me softly.

"So you think that even if I'd had a father, and he was a bad father, I'd still grieve for a good father. You seem like you've been a good father."

"My kids made me into a good father; I didn't start out that way. I'd be good now from the beginning but I don't get that chance."

I shut my eyes for a moment. I'm wondering if my mom feels that way, whether she can help me avoid feeling that way. I never thought that seeing my father's face here in this tiny room would make me see my mother's face, where she is now, I imagine, in that old patched La-Z-Boy with a book propped on a pillow and a bag of Hershey's kisses to crinkle through.

"Try not to be too hard on your mother. Not much was openly discussed in those days. You can imagine I've kept up on the subject. And not only because I advise couples with fertility problems. It's beginning to change. At some clinics, the donors authorize release of their names and addresses to the children when they're eighteen. Of course they can't be minors or there'd be legal paternity issues. I was such a youngster when I did it. No idea really. It was good pay for a scholarship boy. I'd like to paint myself in some altruistic light, tell you it meant something to me that there was a family out there someplace raising a child they otherwise couldn't have. But I was so tired I was numb most of the time, and it was a meal ticket to me then, in my exhaustion, just another bodily fluid. I don't mean to hurt your feelings. I'm sure your mother wanted you very much."

"I was a meal ticket. And what am I now?"

"Just who you are. Though I don't think I can invite you into the bosom of the family. I don't have that sort of modern sensibility."

"I know that. I mean, you're single, so I have an urge to introduce you to my mother but it would never work out."

He started laughing. "Thank you. I'm flattered."

"She might not be. She doesn't like men much."

"What about the father of your baby. Where's he in the picture?"

"I don't know. I don't know if he's in the picture. Maybe that's why I had to find you."

"Well, he doesn't know what he's missing. That's all. And maybe he'll wake up to it one day."

While my father goes to ask one of his partners to examine me, I sit in the room alone, facing down the instruments on the metal tray, feeling their chill and longing for the chaotic world where germs thrive. I wrap my arms around my belly, around this baby I'm certain is a girl. I let myself envision the delivery and Nigel is there. He is there when she comes into the world and opens her fearless eyes upon him, and I watch him take up her kicking body and hold her close to him, bring her to the beating warmth of his own. I know that he will go down the hall with her to the place of further testing, a room again like this, where he will volunteer himself to feel her pain wholly even as he can't feel mine. These are the things that will make him her father and she won't have to grow up in a world devoid of good men, perhaps even a world I have made devoid of good men.

At the bus station, my father told me about the people I come from. Irish Coal miners from West Virginia. Polish steel workers from Chicago. Later teachers, preachers, and doctors. *If I tell you your great great grandfather drove a jitney or that your great grandmother spoke Menominee and Chippewa or that your great aunt was a physical therapist who worked with convalescing soldiers, I can only give you the sketchiest details. The rest you have to fill in with literature, history, biography, or your imagination, like anybody else.*

I thought about how we looked later. Like a father and a daughter saying goodbye . . . I don't think more awkward in our embrace than anyone else of our age and time. He bought my ticket and pressed forty dollars into my hand as I was about to board. *Count it*, he said softly. It was the exact sum he'd told me he was paid for being a donor. I guess he couldn't find another way to give me cash. *Tell your mother I was an altruistic guy.* His smile was faint; he held it there till it looked half grimace. He didn't stand and wave. He ducked away face downwards so I had no last look. Did he think I would cry less that way? Was he suddenly ashamed? I was going home with a whole new set of questions.

XII.

On the way home. The foothills of the Cascades. Apple orchards in shadow, thunderheads spilling over the ridges above. Hypnotic rows of trees. The *fut fut fut* of the irrigation birds, the spray opalescent in the westering sun, the sound of crickets and evening doves coming up at dusk. Abandoned houses with branches out their chimneys. Barns pulled down by blackberries. Then black and purple buttes, chewed down brush and sage, dolomite shining beneath dry grass. Altitude sun that bakes cedar sap. Cirques full of snow. Steep, so steep it makes the weight of your body drop through your windpipe. Then it's down, down, and down. The coastal farmlands are dusted in a fine grain of color, paprika and curry.

I see tanker cars black in the sun, fat belly after fat belly beneath rows of shimmering poplar trees. The lumber towns reek of mill sewage, harboring pools of rottenness in syrup form somewhere out of sight. In sight, the original magnate's Victorian mansion and downtown the recent addition of a chainsaw Indian. I know these towns.

She cried when I called. Neither of us want to fight anymore. My mother and I seem to have a mechanism between us, a winch wound too tight that suddenly hurtles its line. On the phone she mentioned Frank. I keep trying out his name as though I could make it ring with familiarity. *Frank.* Trusting her to trust herself. I talked about the baby. *The baby. Frank.* Will the new cogs alter the old mechanism?

I told her about hearing the baby's heartbeat amplified: *pong, pong.* Like a badminton birdie whiffling back and forth over a net—aloft, aloft—hurrying up to my heartbeat. She was excited about searching garage sales for Johnny-jump-ups and crib gyms and changing tables, an inventory that seemed overwhelming. She asked about my father, but I heard a different tone in her voice, a longing to be spared. She doesn't want to know enough about him to make him real. Secretly, she must have hoped I'd be rejected by my father, then I could belong to her again. I don't think she's capable of understanding that he might mean something to me apart from her. It's enough that she could understand that with Nigel. Enough for me.

Instead of telling her about my father, I told her a story she'd long ago told me. My mother once found a locket that her grandfather had given her grandmother; it had been stolen years before. She was at an "estate sale" of goods, aisle upon aisle, booth after booth and yet she was drawn to the table where lay the locket: 24 karat gold filigree with a tiny ruby. It had once held the photo of her grandfather, but of course was now empty. My mother couldn't afford to buy it, but she told the woman its origin and let her know that she was displaying stolen property. The woman countered: "There were lots of lockets in this style."

"That may be so," said my mother, "but I bit this one when I was eight-years-old, and here on the back is the mark from my tooth."

I told her that what I have now is like that toothmark— a moment of recognition. Indisputable.

Close to home. The tree farms that link the inland towns to the coast are all new green, a raw, discomfiting color like the pink of scar tissue that comes after a surface burn. But it's not long to the peninsula. If you know to look for it, the light changes first. You can see it on the sky, the way the river opens like a valve to reflection, joining the bay, while the land narrows and loops, west and north. The bay's curve and lambent shape suggest an intimate familiar between breast and arm, a ladle of comfort. At least that's how I feel about it now, picturing my mother at the station, rocking up on the balls of her feet and squinting to try and spot me.

. . . AND OTHER TALES OF MODERN FAMILY

In Refrain

Moss on the rooftops is the only greening thing of this season. Wood smoke chugs from the chimneys without making a difference to the sky: gray, gone gray, all gray. Every leaf has fallen from the apple tree. Clusters of apples cling close to the trunk, and the brown of the branches quivers like a violin next to a young girl's cheek. Blots of brightness held aloft, another smatter of color rotting on the ground. I fill my pockets, a woman no longer young, looking like someone's wife except she isn't someone's wife and for her it's twilight not suppertime and she's alone on a road on an island floating in a sea, it doesn't matter where, it's all one sea and somewhere there is another woman, her mother, bundled and walking alone. I polish the apples with my muffler, readying in my mind the wooden bowl where I will make the colors sing the image in refrain. It sings now still, this song for my brother, strains of a violin aching like tree limbs in the wind.

The moon when she comes is not kind. She takes a shaving off the landscape with the lens of her eye. Nothing is so black and white as the shadow of a man sliding across a picket fence. Even though the man is my neighbor I take to the house; the shadow he owns tonight is gargantuan. All the dogs take up the chorus, all the dogs laugh when she does. The moon has smeared lips; she pours my drink.

Your hands are scarred by metal and your clothes smell of engine oil, do you make anything of this? I always ask you because I know you don't and then things can just be themselves again as they are to you and I sleep better. I know I am too old for this. Don't worry. Jack will return soon and I won't call and for a time it will be all right. I count the times you cut me or bruised me. A brother's love.

There's no man on earth I'd laugh about this for, except you. Your need to hurt me was the need to hurt me first, before anyone else could, because you felt the inevitability of it. And afterwards your ministrations were so tender, coaching me in lessons of survival. I count memories on an abacus, not for totals, but because I need to give the numbers weight and sound. *Clack* and *Smack*, I redeliver the blows.

I still cannot stand to be too happy. Like the hummingbirds at the window sill, their beaks stuck in the too sweet syrup, I whiffle my feathers against the air, batting atoms at ecstasy, returning but never staying at the source. Love is for me a nervous disorder; it makes my hands shake.

I'm older. My memories are out of order. My mind shuffles without grace, a newcomer at this table. I have someone now. Jack has put a stretch of time between me and all those others, those days and nights, to the next to the next to the next, one ticket one round, one ticket one ride, torn ticket stubs, half names, half numbers. Try to remember. Give gills to the snake, wings to the wolf. The lamb bleats with a forked tongue. Men call, years later, to tell me that I really meant something to them. They want to know if my hair is still long.

The succession has stopped succeeding, like escalator stairs that lower their teeth and disappear. I have chosen a man who leaves me on a regular basis. His profession, my safeguard.

Sometimes we can't talk and I am grateful. He doesn't exacerbate my discontent. I study the way our shoes have fallen on the floor. One clog lies sideways on the oriental rug, a capsized boat, buffeted by pattern and filling; the other moored in the corner. Jack's boots dropped side by side tilt on uneven heels away from each other.

We nap, stir, stretch, lap at each other like kittens. Love unconscious dreaming. We are buoys bobbing under and out to a wind of two breaths.

You help girls. You unclog carburetors, hook up water heaters, build dog kennels, loan tuition money, drill in deadbolts and don't fall in love. You climb in and out of beds wondering if you've done anyone a favor. You're still thinking about the woman you saw at the phone company, years ago, the day you waited in three lines. You waited in front of her. You waited behind her. You fell in love with the way she carried her body, as though she would own it always. You don't want to know her. You want to watch her in line after line, unconscious of what it is you are waiting for.

We were traded as children, though I don't know what went into the bargain. I try to imagine our two grandmothers together, one gaining and one giving up children, one elegant and spare with legs made for waltzing, the other stout with hands of care swollen around her wedding bands. We were children of parents who had split, were splitting themselves again with new people somewhere far away. You stood in the shuttered study, spinning the globe, spinning it, spinning it.

There were so many systems to learn and everywhere we walked we walked around her. Our father's mother. She closed sandwich bags with wooden clothes pins, arranged camelias in vases, kumquats in bowls. We were good children and suffered her arrangement. She taught you to play cards. She showed me her high school yearbook and turning the pages told me who was dead and who was living and I looked closely at the youthful faces there as though I could detect the difference. We weeded in her garden and she paid us a penny a weed. We had to count the weeds. I don't remember more. Except that I was glad to leave. The darkness in her house was an olive green, hard green, green that lives in shadow and smells like linen in an old woman's closet.

I remember your bright voice in the morning air, the seriousness with which you snapped on your seatbelt at our grandmother's request, then turned to the back seat and made sure that I obeyed yours. I looked out the window and let the neighborhoods slide by, expecting from the car the same calm disinterest I'd felt when the airplane wheels left the runway in Germany. I prepared for air, for clouds, for more of nothing while you displayed an alertness that, if those who look for early signs are right, showed you were the one who bore the burden of mistrust. You watched for freeway signs and asked about distances, for all I know, you memorized the way back.

"Here fishy, fishy."

I ignored you. I was curled up in the wing chair in my grandfather's study. It was a black, massive, patent leather beast with brass rivets, relic of a time when rooms were made to be masculine or feminine. My bare legs stuck to its glossy surface and I slid into my grandfather's deep dent. The footstool curled back like a genie's slipper. The wallpaper vine curved and twisted on the walls, its leaves delicately shaded in near perfect realism. The card table bore a petit point mandala of geometric design and its feet were bronze bird claws clutching globes of solid glass. On it lay an elephant tusk, elaborately scrimshawed, two rows of holes marking its purpose as a scoreboard. I marched the pegs up and down, first mother, then father: mother father mother father.

On the mantel stood a collection of old piggy banks, the hunter who stood erect with a penny balanced on the barrel, the bird whose wings opened at the shot and drop of the coin; at the other end a heavy forlorn Negro head who lifted the penny to his lips and swallowed with a roll of his eyes. I was cranking the hand up to his lips when I heard your voice again, in the front hall.

"Here fishy, fishy."

Just tall enough to hold the fishing rod over the banister, you smile at me as you bounce the line. I let you make me want the hook, round like a dandelion, composed of many barbs. It isn't enough to invite me, you have to make me want it. I am beguiling even then, holding out the skirt of my pinafore, twirling beneath your hook . . . maybe, maybe not. "Fishy," you call, sing-songing it, "fishy, let me catch you." I take it in the fullness of my lower lip, feel the thin barbs catch, sting and tug. I may have cried when my grandfather removed it, but what I remember is the beseeching tone in your voice. It is the tone I've responded to in other men's voices, the hook that cannot be cut out.

I liked Angelina's voice; I always associated it with the warm sugar smell of cakes baking. I liked her mouth full of turned teeth and black gaps and gold. The house belonged to my grandmother, but the kitchen was Angelina's. She named the animals: the dog was Blackie, the cat was Whitey, nobody thought anything of it. Maybe she told her friends and they laughed at us. I don't know. I had never seen a black person before I met her. She reached her hand towards me and I took it and licked it firmly from one side to the other. Then I heard her laugh. "She thinks I'm chocolate!" I didn't think she was chocolate, but something about her had permitted it. You hung back, watching. I didn't know anything about watching. I wanted to reach out and taste people.

I was about five then, almost as tall as the fifty pound bag of dog food on the back porch, which I regularly dipped into. You found that it wasn't hard to persuade a sister who ate dog kibble to eat snail pellets. You told me they were tootsie rolls.

I never thought you were cruel, and I don't believe you are now. I cried when I heard you being spanked. I crept in your bed that night and you put your arms around me even as you slept. What I remembered was the jagged spoon the doctor held out to me, shadowing it with his other hand. The edge was serrated, all the way around. My first impression of calculated cruelty. I don't know what he would have done if I hadn't swallowed the root-bitter syrup. My grandmother waited in the waiting room. I took it solemnly. The belly of the spoon was smooth and familiar against my tongue; the ridges of the spoon tickled at the corners of my mouth.

You told me we had to let some blood out of my swollen finger. It was turning purple; there was a red line beneath the tin ring, the juice can poptop my grandmother had told me not to put on. I did it because I was marrying in my mind, one day forever . . . a home . . . not a man. I couldn't construct a man's face that was fantasy, but I unpacked my home from a suitcase, at the end of a road, miles of jet black, smooth as silk stockings. And my face was not womanly, nor beautiful, nor my mother's blanched by the camera's flash. It was my infant face—bald sleep creased moon. For years, I wore a found key around my neck on a ribbon, so I could be always, anywhere, knowing and going home.

But the finger was dying, and you told me we had to let some blood out. We got up early and padded down the halls of the ticking house. I never questioned our secrecy. You knew more about me than the adults. Your solutions never meant leaving me.

The kitchen is filled with the damp shadow of the garden. The sharpest knife is the biggest knife. You tell me to stare at something, the blue glow of the pilot lights in the black stove. I offer my hand on the cutting board. My mind offers my body for sacrifice. My body would have offered my mind. The body has an intelligence of its own. The body wields fear. I pull away. I pull all four fingers across the blade.

Sometimes I am able to draw people to me. They see an unusual animatedness and mistake it for beauty. I sweep them into my sorrow. It's all so operatic, singing at knife point like Madame Butterfly, holding the blade there yourself. Still I cry when I hear that music. I do.

It happens. The heart becomes swollen from too much blood in it, constricted by some pain, banded round its beating part. We don't want to die, just let some blood out.

When I saw my mother again, she was spotted, head to foot pink blotches like the marks left by kisses or pinches or bites. She'd developed an allergy to everything, not only the foreign land and man she'd been in, with, within, but to eggs and sunlight and elastic. I didn't see the blotches as marks on her skin. I saw them as wounds beneath the skin, visible because her skin had thinned, etiolated, turned translucent. And whatever it was that was wounding her, it was everywhere. We couldn't protect her.

The disease vindicated her family and they paid for it—

doctors, tests—the university medical center tracing it to a microbe created when the bacteria of a Mexican fish combined with the plaque of her teeth. In the mornings, she cut up my banana, glaring at the newspaper her father used to shield himself, looking at me when he lowered it. In the afternoons, she came home with needle marks up and down the pale insides of her arms. She came home punctured. Her family felt it was fitting punishment. No one ever said so: condemnation served up with their concern. She had to swallow.

My father had told her that what she knew with her senses was untrue. The body went on with its signals, wielding fear. She had her affair in the open, in the emptiness, the place swept clean of despair. It didn't help to show my father his cowardice. If he could kill her, he wanted her back.

The heart gone black. Victory so often means alone . . . only alone. She took us in her arms and told us we were hers always, she was ours always. Could we believe her? She is still waiting to hear us say yes, even now, yes.

I don't know if children are cruel or if they act in protest, wishing to be sent back to a place they have a nascent memory of, and killing . . . it's curiosity about the passage. I had a small Susie Homemaker oven for baking Small Susie Homemaker cakes that never rose to the satisfying heights of those Angelina made. It came with a viewer window big enough for two children to look through if they put their heads side by side, which is what my brother and I did, making audible gasps as we watched our offering of insects and slugs shrivel on a bed of kitty litter.

My mother became a secretary and rented us a small house. We learned to hurry. We drank blender breakfasts of Tiger's Milk, bananas and raw eggs. They were still sliding down our throats as we rode the school bus. Sometimes long strings of egg white, stretching, dropping all of sudden into a bulge and quivering at stomach bottom.

Her parents sent over men who smelled like ice buckets: maraschino sweet, fumy and moist. She went out with each one once. While she was on the telephone, she drew question marks on a note pad. Then she would turn the pad upside down. *Turn a question mark upside down, hook yourself.*

My mother's loneliness was violent. She clenched her teeth on it. *I am not . . . grunt, strain, sweat . . . lonely.* She inflicted activity on the world. When vines threatened to tug our little house down by one corner, she bought an electric chainsaw. I watched her slash through the mess, watched the loosed snarl slide from the roof and wrestle with my mother. She came up waving the saw, hacking with a vengeance, severing every vine, kicking the tangle from her feet, whirling around to take the devil's tail, cutting clean through the cord itself. Silence. Finale. She always laughed then.

At the river, we made up rhymes. *Pollywogs, almost frogs.* In the spring, the banks had flooded. *All one leggy, all one army.* The waters had receded, leaving pools on the land, pools full of stranded creatures. *Little huddle in the puddle.* My mother walked from puddle to river bank, refilling the wine bottle with water, pouring into the puddle, while we squatted in the mud drawing her initials.

On dead days, we could change the radio station as often as we wanted. On dead days, she lay on the beach with her feet splayed. Every so often, we ran our fingernails along the insides of her arches. She kicked and mumbled. On dead days, we rubbed her: four little hands and a bottle of sun block. Then we let her sleep and hoped that when her body filled back up with a person, it would be the person we wanted back.

Once a man in a black Speedo came and threw the stick for our dog. Each time, we watched to see how far our dog could swim. Each time, the man turned to see if our mother had moved. We had put mussel shells over her eyes as sunguards.

"What time do you eat lunch?"

"When she wakes up," we said.

The man moved off down the beach, not far, settling against a log that gave him us for a view. We moved into the shade under the umbrella. You blew up my beach ball. The man was standing, leaning against the log.

Your breath hisses and echoes inside the plastic, then stops, suddenly, as you pinch off the nipple and narrow your eyes. I look then too. The man has himself out, is pumping his penis like a jack handle. I expect him to grow taller. Our dog is standing at attention, whining, wagging wildly, waiting for the man to stop shaking his stick, waiting for him to pull off his penis and throw it. "Fetch it!" we shout, sending the dog at a dead run. "Fetch it!"

My father surfaced and requested us. The letters he'd sent were loving, longing, full of deprivation. *Wars on foreign shores keep me from your arms.* I made them up. Wars and letters.

My mother always sent us with gifts, tins full of German Christmas cookies, bags of coffee, dried figs, avocados. She sent gifts to placate an angry god. The possibility of reviving his sadness made her feel safe.

She would walk us onto the plane . . . the days before security gates. Once she was too long in saying goodbye and they had to lower the stair again to let her off. She chatted with the man next to us as she waited for the door to become stairs again and I saw how she was for a whole weekend without us. She tickled the air with her laughter and he strained against his seat belt to join her, and she made him feel she was brave by amusing him with our hardships. More kisses for us and she vanished with a hydraulic hiss.

We forgot our parents as fast as we could and busied ourselves with what everything would do at our command. Foldout trays, flip-up ashtrays, lean-back seats. I tried to stick my bubble gum onto the air nozzle. My brother leaned down and let the avocados go, one by one, to see if they would roll to the back of the plane.

I slept on a couch at my father's, near a window overlooking a bunch of wounded trees. He had many hobbies and many children, taken up and put aside, with regularity, only then I didn't have the vantage point of a lifespan. And

I didn't make the connection between my stepmother's silences and my father's profusion of hobbies.

Incisions and leaking sap, props and slippages, bound limbs and green stumps, all so he could pick two fruits from one tree. I didn't make any connections back then. I walked with clumps of leaves in my arms to his burning pile and we made the day grayer.

Everywhere in that house, interruption was imminent. Someone might come upon me, remind me that I did not belong in that place. It was the way my stepsister went quickly to the piano bench, and lifting its lid took a sheaf of music or some mysterious notebook; it was in the quick look she gave me, that clicking shut of herself as audible as the lid meeting the latch.

The kitchen overlooked the den, the hallway was open to the living room. Anyone on their way from one end of the house to the other made me shift and twist, wondering whose chair it was I sat in.

I liked my father's workbench out in the garage, a surface of incongruent tools and materials, evidence of the last project merging with the next. He was a finisher of things, but he had a borrower's mind. He switched subjects in search of transformation; the balsa wood airplane suggested the next limb of the Bonsai, the Bonsai needles a setting for the tiger's eye in silver, so on and so on.

I would stand out there while he was at work, feeling the coldness of the cement even through the crepe soles of my shoes, flipping the handle of the vice and watching the weighted end drop. I was not aware of wrongs done to me, only his loneliness out there with the diesel and dung smell of the lawn mower and the coldness spreading in his arches, and my sure-feeling that if he were with us, his projects would have had a place, he would have been warm and watched over.

Red blotches floating on gray. Why not boats on blue? Why not black on snow? Even so it's mine, I can't alter memory. My childhood is locked in one season. Red dress, gray sky, I'm up on a fence. Tree branches, black scratches against the sky. All the bark is wet. Wood smoke thins, thickens, wends its way around the trunks, whispering, all the time, whispering about dying.

You and the neighbor child are far ahead. I cried getting up on the fence, and I bunged one knee, and I left scuff marks on the mossy wood. You straddle it, moving along by rocking up onto your hands and swinging your legs forward. My spit is thick with rage, and when words come out they skid on the air, too fast, too loud. You don't look back. You don't wait. I stiffen my arms and lock my elbows, getting ready.

My father's eyes are hazel limned by a silver line. Close up, very close up, like islands of earth floating in a sea of ice. He is that close to me, extracting splinters from my thighs. He could hold his hands so still. I remember the steadiness of his hands. Staring at them made the walls of the room ripple. The half-moons of his fingertips looked like the tips of petals, purest white.

His face was dignified by the moment of consummate attention. I had never seen him before without his sadness, and my amazement made the pain seem very far away, a siren coming through a pinhole, high pitched but stretched very thin. His sadness was the way he sat in that house with his knees together and his feet apart, the way his socks wrinkled around his ankles and there wasn't enough hair to comb across his head; it was the way he stopped hugging me before I could really get inside his hug . . . all those little warning pats. But his face was flushed now with concentration and his hands were so still, and he was so skillful at this, minimizing pain as he caused it, that I wished there was some other part of myself I could offer up for hurting.

She beat her hands against the steering wheel. "I hate everybody, I hate everything, I hate the world." I looked at the circular fracture lines my head had made in the windshield. I was still gripping my school books in my lap. *No two snowflakes are alike.*

"Mother," you said, "Move the car."

She pulled over next to a steak house because it was the first place she saw people. Our car was still making a noise like scales sliding over sand, only it was tires on ice. A man was buying a newspaper from one of the machines. He had a beard, and a face that gave the impression of concavity, not unpleasantly, like a wooden spoon worn palm smooth from much stirring. And he had an accent, maybe Kentucky or Alabama, his words anyway were tacky on his tongue.

He didn't ask her what was the matter. She asked directions. He offered for us to follow him. His "if you like" was swallowed up by the river filling with keeled over corn stalks and busted open pumpkin heads. He was afraid for what some man might have done. He was afraid to harm her with his help.

That simply, that quietly, Russell entered our lives. He had the disposition of a priest in a working man. No labor too low. If they laid him off, if they promoted someone else over him, if he stayed in cold storage till his balls ached, each was an occasion for transcendence. His achievement was humility, but he loved my mother like a jewel, like the heirloom finery of some Charlotte or Scarlet or Odette way back when, reminder of a grander time enacted in his head, something he could sacrifice for. She pawned herself. She had depressions, she had lovers. She allowed him to keep taking her back. Then it didn't matter that she made boeuf bourguignonne to his pot roast. Then she begged him to blow on the spark, begged him not to spit on it.

I had on my party dress, eyelet lace and appliqued swans. Russell let me carry the cake from the car, the cake my grandfather had ordered. I fell flat on my ballerinas, my frothy frosting ladies on toepoint nothing but a mud-chocolate squish.

My noise had no effect on Russell. He was thinking of solutions to mess. He stripped me on the lawn, sashes sodden, bows unstrung. My mother would have sung to me in bubbles, but she was gone. Holding me by one arm, he hosed me off while the dog licked my knees, my sweet knees. Cold water, warm tongue. Russell's fingers left marks on my arms, those red blotches.

You stood in the house and watched. I saw you behind the curtain, and I tried to be the one watching. It was worse to be the one watching.

We were in the pantry with all the food his coupons had bought. Mother and Russell were in the kitchen. He was hitting her with a rolled newspaper. He was whacking her on the head, whacking her with a rolled newspaper like a dog. She was laughing.

"It makes a lot of noise, but it doesn't hurt."

"What does hurt you?"

"Nothing, nothing anymore."

Phwack, laughter, phwack, laughter, phwack. You're there with me, holding a knife, waiting for the first sound that isn't hollow. There are rows and rows of paper towels on the shelf, boxes of macaroni, canned fish.

"Kill him," I whisper.

"Who?" you say, jabbing the air, "Who?"

Then you sink the knife into the belly of a bag of rice and slit it across the bulge. Pearly grains fan out over the floor, like a veil of tears. I am the first to throw them.

I hear the rice pattering on the floor as grains lift off my palms. Your hands are whirling the patterned air. We make a rice storm. *Up coming down coming up coming down.* We're on our hands and knees, scooping it from the floor and flinging it aloft. "Happy New Year!" we scream, "Happy Honeymoon! Bon Voyage!"

The moon when she comes is not kind . . . . She has smeared lips . . . .

She pours my drink.

Riptide

The huge cypress tree was the same, scraggy and black, casting darkness all around itself. Beneath it were the three uneven hummocks that from a distance suggested people sleeping under blankets. A moist draft crept up inside Anthony's trouser legs as he stood looking at the Indian burial mounds. They were ringed by stones and shells . . .the same as could be said of his childhood.

When he was small, his father and three uncles had called themselves the chieftains, and sometimes after family barbecues, they would build a bonfire on the beach and dance in a mock ceremony. He and his cousins would screech and hoot and topple over each other. The men wore towels and seaweed wrapped around their waists, corn husks secured to their heads by string, slashes of lipstick across their cheeks. The chieftains shook their scepters of warped driftwood and commanded silence. "Who knows the secret handshake of the Rincon tribe?" they demanded. And the children pressed their fingers together, thumbs on top, making triangular shapes of their hands. "Then greet your tribesmen!" And the children smacked their cup shaped hands together like the two sides of a clam. "How's the weather?"

"Clammy!" the children shouted in reply.

Every summer the chieftains gave out prizes for the art contest, Japanese scissors and origami kits and cricket cages, sometimes fire crackers and candies. The prizes went to every child who entered, under categories made up for that purpose: best shell mobile, best driftwood rhinoceros, best mermaid mosaic, best shark eggcase collection.

But it was more than what his uncles made of it. Everywhere he and his cousins went, into the slough at night with flashlights to catch bull-frogs or up to the railroad tracks in the fog to break bottles, they felt the presence of the people that came before; they felt the eerie excitement of being watched all the time.

In the field, subdivision markers flagged by bright plastic tape distracted Anthony from his childhood reverie amid eucalyptus trees and pampas grass. He pulled the markers out, one by one, though he knew it wouldn't forestall the final outcome for the land. The backs of his hands were dusted by mustard grass. He chewed a stalk of licorice and spit out the stringy pulp.

The bodies that lay beneath the mounds might now end up with some garbage in a landfill or as build-up for a berm on a freeway. Then he thought about Diana . . .not living but dead, as she was. And he had an image, Diana dug-up, Diana born aloft in the jagged metal shovel of a bulldozer, her bones in a queenly position of recline, one leg fallen over the other, one straight arm touching the lower knee, the whole posture suggesting protection of the center. For a moment, it was too magnificent, the queen raised skyward in a gleaming silver litter; in another moment, too horrible, the machine lurched into gear and the bones fell from each other as they disappeared into a trench. He sat on a log away from the mounds, drawing long breaths, clearing his mind for Lynette, his new wife.

Anthony unlocked the trunk of the car and picked up a sack of groceries. He was about to heft another when he saw his daughter, Annie. She was up on her toes looking in, her chin lifted towards the kitchen window. He could see Lynette inside at the kitchen sink. Annie backed up a few paces and went up on her toes again. Then she padded around the house and disappeared.

He went in the kitchen door, and after he'd set the bags down, kissed Lynette on the back of the neck. She dropped the vegetables in the sink and twisted around suddenly, putting her wet hands on his cheeks. Often she startled him, as she did now. She was a creature who could turn to camouflage (so that in a room he would sometimes read for hours and forget her), like a heron on an overcast day, stick-like, the blue-gray of driftwood, fog, stones and water, then with an abrupt flap of its enormous wings, in motion. She was thin, an angular and awkward woman, awkward in a way that touched him, like an animal caught in some mid-stage of evolution, stuck with many useless characteristics in a new environment.

She turned towards the sink again, but he stood behind her, hugging her for awhile. The house smelled richly of his childhood: musty and metallic like an old range heating up, and something not unpleasantly earthy, like potatoes at the back of a storage bin that have just begun to sprout. He nuzzled behind Lynette's ear and she shut the water off. "What is it?" she asked, laughing. But he didn't answer and she stood still, leaning against him. He wanted to place her in his history, and he couldn't: telling her the story of every rock and tree would not make him see her there. So they stood, she looking down at his hands around her waist, he looking through the kitchen window at the faded wind sock flying from the flag pole, and the blue and white Spanish tiles set into the garden wall, and the pathways of smooth round stones and opaque beach glass that his grandmother had made, and the lemon tree that had split at the base in a storm years ago and grown back together, and the nasturtiums that grew in profusion around totems of driftwood.

When he'd brought the last of the bags in, he remembered Annie.

"She was with the boys a minute ago," Lynette said.

He looked out the living room window and made out Lynette's sons: Marcos and Kyle squatting together around one of the pools left by the low tide, and Randall farther off, staring down pensively at something. Anthony turned to walk down the hall but stopped when he saw the hand prints on the sliding glass door, Annie's size and at her height. He understood then: up on her toes and at the window, circling the house to locate Lynette and avoid her. He imagined how carefully and slowly she'd slid the door open.

"Is she out there?" Lynette called from the kitchen.

"No," he called back, trying to sound casual. "She probably got tired of poking sea anemones with sticks."

Annie was not one of Cupid's dimpled, round-faced cherubs, but Anthony was thankful she was as stubborn and durable as she looked. Her jaw was wide and her chin definite as a thumb print. Her slate green eyes were narrow but long, inquisitive, observant and unsparing. Anthony had had her hair cut short after Diana died. There was such a lot of it. Like her mother, she had a real head of hair. Now cropped in a bowl shape, it was so thick the bangs stood off her forehead, framing her face like a little helmet.

When he came in, she was making one of those pictures that require most of a box of crayolas: a coating of black over a garish assortment of colors, then a pin to scratch lines through the first layer of paraffin.

"Hi Daddy," she said, without looking up.

He sat down on the end of the bed and watched her applying black crayon with great force. After a few strokes she stopped and leaned against his leg, gazing at him.

"It's going to be pretty," he said.

"It's going to be for you."

"Lucky me," he said, adding quietly, "Didn't you have a nice time with the boys?"

She shrugged and turned back to her picture. "They do the same things over and over."

He smiled, looking at the back of her head and shaking his own. She would do better at battling adult banality.

"I put all my clothes in one drawer," she announced.

"Why'd you do that, pumpkin?"

"It smells like mommy."

"Show me," he said, and they went together to the chest of drawers, and she lifted the shelf paper from one corner and showed him the fine dusting of Jean Nate powder that lay beneath. He felt like picking up the chest of drawers and throwing it into the sea. Instead he picked up a handful of Annie's clothes and pressed them to his face.

"C'mon" Annie said, as she sat back down to her artwork, "This is the good part."

He closed his eyes against memory and heard Diana anyway, pounding down the hall on her heels. He saw her come in as she once had, at this time of day, in this light, standing at the end of the bed with her feet planted far apart, shouting at him: "You shut out everything! You shut me out!" Then he heard doors in the house being wrenched open, slammed shut . . . Annie's baby cries. He sympathized with the house, ransacked by her rage. The force wasn't necessary. Doors could be easily sprung by a thumb and two fingers, swing free suddenly, make a breeze and relieve your clothes of their stiffness. Doors you could put a shoulder to, give a good leaning to, press in on the knob and lift the tongue past the warped latch. But with her, doors were either open or closed. When she challenged him, he could feel all his weight pitch against the surface she was pounding on, and it seemed to him now that the two of them had been unable to know each other. And he hadn't shut her out, he just couldn't come at things dead-on.

His body filled with an ache that backed up inside him like smoke and pressed against the top of his throat as though it were a damper thrown closed. The entire time she'd beat on the front door, the back had stood wide open . . . wide open. If she'd whispered his name in the dark, even once, whispered it.

Annie was pulling on his fingers, complaining.

"I only get one black crayola in the box and it's the one I use the most."

Anthony stood in the living room, in the dark, listening. The seals wouldn't quit their barking. Voices so hoarse and full, hearing them made him hear again the cello sonatas Diana used to play. He smiled, remembering how the cats used to come sneaking back in after the weekly house cleaning, skulking and looking left and right. One seal's voice asserted itself over the rest, on and on: an aria, a solo, a lost love. Anthony didn't know why he was up.

Lynette's sand dollars were spread out all over the coffee table. She spent hours drilling holes in them with a needle and threading dental floss through so that they could hang as ornaments in the Christmas tree. How like Lynette, making this a memory now so that it could be stored up and then brought out again at Christmas and the memory of their first Christmas together joined to it. They needed a new reserve of memory, both of them.

He told himself to go to bed but didn't make a move. Late at night, he and Diana had fought. Towards the end, he often stayed up alone, wondering when enough would be enough, or what, and wondering if it would come in a terrible exhalation of silence.

He sat down on the cold hearth stones and closed his eyes. Annie loved the seals. There was an enormous one the surfers fed sandwiches. It would swim up the beach while he and Annie walked, and back with them when they turned round. The seal would swoop beneath the surface, and Annie would sing a few lines of her seal song, and then they'd spot his head coming up again just beyond the breakers.

This summer, she wore her grandmother's wide brim straw hat everywhere . . . stubbed toes, protruding belly and the huge pink hat. She'd pestered him about the seal while he was cleaning up breakfast, and he'd told her she could go to the edge of the property and look. Coming in to clear plates from the table, he'd stood for a moment and watched her climb over the thick ice plant and up the dunes, the tutu skirt of her swimsuit lifting and falling. She'd glanced quickly at the house, where reflections on the sliding glass doors prevented her from seeing him, then turned back to the seal, pulling off the hat in one hand and waving grandly.

The next morning, Anthony heard the boys' voices carried on the wind as he walked. A tiger shark's tail left cross hatches in the sand as it thrashed and snapped at the three boys jumping around it.

"Grab its tail!" shouted Marcos, still holding the rod.

"No way. You do it." Randall, the middle brother, shook his hands in excitement as he side-stepped the shark.

"Chicken shits!" Marcos yelled. He dropped to his knees, frantically digging at the sand to make a place for the rod. "Kyle," he shouted, "get over here and hold the rod."

"No," the youngest boy wailed, transfixed by the eyes of the shark that threatened a malevolence worse than his brother's.

"Here, I'll do it," said Randall, scampering in a wide circle around the fish which twisted like a lash.

But before he arrived at his brother's side, the line

broke, and Anthony saw all three boys look up at the filament floating in the air.

"He's loose!" shrieked Kyle, running for higher, drier sand.

Marcos dropped the rod and charged the shark. He grabbed it by the tail and as its head jerked back towards him, he wrenched it into the air and began to spin. He whipped round and round, sighting off the end of the animal's flat snout, letting its weight hold him upright as he increased speed.

Randall hugged himself in fear. Kyle was the first to turn and look down the beach, secretly hoping for adult intervention. "Geezer Noise is coming," shouted Kyle, making a move in Anthony's direction before he remembered himself and stopped.

Marcos let go of the shark, sending it skittering over the hard sand. He ran after it, his body zigzagging after his head as though he were diving through the air. By the time Anthony arrived, he was standing over the shark, feet spread apart, breathing hard. Kyle was the first to greet his stepfather, gibbering in his high-pitched voice about Marcos' heroics.

Randall stood at a distance watching Anthony pick up the rod and blow sand out of the reel.

"Well, what have you got here?"

Marcos looked up and squinted, a calculated moment, as though he needed time to recognize Anthony. "What's it look like?" he said, sneering, and then abashed at his own arrogance, he added, "Good thing we put fifty pound test on the rod this morning."

Holding the rod in front of him, Anthony replied, "It's going to take a good part of the evening to get the sand out of this reel." Then surprised at the edge in his voice, he reminded himself: they're just boys.

Marcos stared at the shark, which lay dazed and convulsing in the sand. Randall still had his arms crossed. To Anthony, Randall's whole body belied waiting, waiting to decide with whom he should ally himself. The silence mounted and Kyle blurted out, "Isn't he a beaut?"

"Yes," said Anthony, hoping he could win Marcos with

a little admiration. "That's a good-size tiger shark, must have put up quite a fight."

"Yeah, sure did," said Marcos. "We were all three on the rod at one point." And then he checked himself, kicking the sand.

"Look at the markings on him," chirped Kyle, "just like the decals on my Tiger Fighter."

Anthony's ears filled with the racket of sea gulls and waves breaking and for a moment he couldn't think of what it was the boy was talking about. Then he remembered the shelf of prized model airplanes and turned his attention back to the boys.

"What do you want to do with it?"

"Keep it," said Marcos before the others could answer.

"What for?" Anthony asked, unable to keep from smiling.

"As a trophy. You know, like deer heads on the wall."

Kyle watched the shark gasp and shiver, watched its mouth open and close, and the magnitude of Marco's suggestion dawned on him. "But then it will have to die."

"So what. It's a mean old shark," said Marcos, sounding less sure of himself.

Anthony decided to opt for practical considerations, aware that an appeal to mercy with Marcos would only get him labeled "panty waist."

"If you want to make it a trophy, you'll have to pay to have it done."

"Naw," said Marcos. "I'll just let it dry out."

Anthony couldn't keep from laughing. "It would stink to high heaven first."

"Let's put it back," whined Kyle, who couldn't stand to look at it anymore and couldn't take his eyes off it.

The shark's skin had gone from sheen to mat. A strip of eel grass was pasted to its belly.

"No," shouted Marcos, stamping his foot in the sand. "It's mine. You leave it right there. I'm going to ask Mother if I can keep it."

Anthony watched the animal's belly pulse, wanting all of a sudden to make Marcos gut it, remembering the first fish he ever slit, instructed by an uncle to punch the blade into the soft place. He hadn't expected the life inside to have so much color: bile and blood, yellows, reds and blues on a palette of slime.

He stood to his full height, dreading the role of disciplinarian, a voice in him saying, "Go ahead, let your mother deal with you," only he knew chances were good that she'd send Marcos back and let him have the final word. He warred with himself over this, whether she was in fact right in asking him to assume a fatherly role, or if it was simply a way to avoid becoming the target of hostility herself.

Randall, until now silent, was the one who settled the matter. Of the three, he was the most reserved and deliberate.

"Marcos," he said, not avoiding his brother's wrathful look, "you know she'll just agree."

Marcos snorted heat and sand from his nose, furious at his brother for assuming the authority he felt he had wrested from his stepfather. "Well shit," he said, turning his back on them all and stalking off down the beach.

Anthony picked up the shark and hurled it back into the sea. Then he watched Marcos' skinny figure recede, scuffing up sand with his feet, shoulder blades sticking out like folded wings.

Marcos had been his paper boy, the reason he'd met Lynette, and nearly not married her. But he had, and he told himself things were loosening up. The boy displayed a willfulness that Anthony was sure, on good days, portended great success; on bad days, a juvenile felon record. He'd reasoned with Marcos, joked with him, shouted at him from the front door, tipped him at the bottom of the driveway, and always the same slick assurance: "No problem, guy." In six months, he'd dug the paper out of the rhododendron bushes, retrieved its soggy remnants from the gutter, hunted for it in his backyard, replaced his television aerial.

"Never have I found it at my door," he told the business office. They claimed no similar complaints had been made. Then, early one summer morning, a tall ash blond stepped from her car, walked to his door and dropped the paper beneath his mail slot. For three days he watched her. He was up at that hour. Annie had to be fed and dressed and readied for Mrs. Hargrove, and he usually did a few hours of computer drafting before driving to the tool and die plant to meet with the other engineers. On the fourth morning, he turned the Levelor blinds horizontal, though it increased the glare on his computer terminal, and waited for her reaction to seeing him. She smiled and waved, then ascended the steps without hurry.

He nearly fell over the phone cord getting to the door, but by the time it swung open, he knew what he was going to say: "Where's Marcos?"

Marcos was at his father's for a month. "We're divorced," she hastened to add, and it started that simply, the exchange of stories about single parenthood. He described to her the difficult early years, his dilemma in restaurants with Annie who declared she couldn't pee with strangers.

"Try finding a sitter for three boys when you've got a bath tub full of lizards," she said. "Try going on a date with them." She laughed and added, "The boys, not the lizards."

So he told her about having someone to dinner with Annie, and all her stuffed animals at the table, and the way she sucked her thumb while rubbing an old pair of Carter's cotton underwear over her lip.

"My youngest kisses the dog, right on his black hairy mouth. It doesn't matter what I say. He loves him."

She leaned against the door frame, and he admired the ease with which she laughed. That weekend, he brewed a whole pot of coffee, and quit the click and hum of his computer for the garden full of bird sounds and Lynette's laughter.

When they started back down the beach, he recognized Lynette far ahead—the bright pattern of her suited shape against the colored square of her towel. Randall and Kyle kept to the water's edge, apart from him. Anthony watched Lynette set aside her magazine and get Marcos a sandwich from the ice chest. She bent from the waist, holding out first one sandwich then another, and Anthony's eyes lingered over the backs of her brown legs. At three that morning, he had awakened swollen as a summer squash against the small of her back. She was like sun-warmed ground. His arms wrapped around her waist, he pressed the curve of himself into the curve of her lower back, and believed he dreamt. Soon he was fully awake, amazed that desire, like pain, could wake him. In her sleep, she made noises like little birds, and even sleeping, opened to him.

She'd been a bit cranky that morning, gathering up the paraphernalia of children, packing the lunch, finding the sun screen, the tar-remover, the mattress patching kit, but he could hardly blame her. *Family vacation.* As he fed the dog, and took out the trash, and started the dishwasher, he marveled at the contradiction in terms. Still, nearly every night, just before they fell asleep, Lynette would whisper to him, "Thank you again." It had gotten so he mocked her, sometimes saying, "thank *you* again," and starting the love-making all over, but secretly it pleased him. She'd cried when he offered to rent the beach house from his uncle. She said she couldn't remember when she and the boys had had a real vacation.

It was Annie that he worried about. At night, she would carry her dozen-odd stuffed animals up to bed and tuck them in. Folding back the spread, she covered them, and said goodnight to each by name. Her animal family. It seemed to him that she felt more family in their odd assortment than in the arrangement he'd created. He hoped he hadn't been too hard on her last night.

Sometimes he wished Lynette would make a special effort, but in this he wasn't sure he knew best. Children sense artificiality so keenly. Perhaps it was right to let things happen naturally. Sometimes, when he and Lynette were up watching TV, he'd find Annie curled up on the floor of the hall with her blanket, as though she needed to hear their voices and feel their closeness but feared to enter in. He would pick her up then and carry her to bed, and the softness of her cheek against his would stir in him an unbearable tenderness.

Later, in the dark of their bedroom, he smelled Lynette's body oil floating slick and warm on the cedar scented dampness of the house; her heat and her rustling displaced the pocket of cold shut-in air where he coiled beneath the covers. He shamed himself in the dark, not answering to his name, trapping her wrists in his hands and pushing them up her back. She would not fight him, and afterwards he would stroke her lightly as though he could give her new skin to live in.

"It's loss that makes you cruel," she would tell him. "I'm not going to leave."

He would reciprocate in whispers, knowing even as he gave them—reassurances, apologies—that it was an adult bedtime story. He was the teller, left to find his own way to dreams. He got up to urinate and then stood in the doorway, staring at the gently sloping mound of blankets on the bed, the wind chime in the garden striking a melody aimless and insistent. He walked down the hall. In the boys' rooms, the shadows cri crossed the floor, feeding darkness to the hummock shap of bodies beneath blankets. He stood before Annie's door, listening for breath, hearing only waves and wind chimes.

Once when e was lying under the car in the garage changing the o , he'd overheard a conversation between Annie and Kyl They came in to get popsicles from the freezer and st d a moment ripping the wrappers off. "What happene to your mother?" Kyle asked, and from the way he whispe d, Anthony knew he'd been forbidden to ask.

"She died i the war," said Annie boldly.

"Really," s d Kyle, sounding impressed, and then they had gone out, aving Anthony feeling as if he were frozen to a sheet of dr ice. Her explanation was as accurate as any he could think f.

"Hiya," sa Lynette to him and the boys. "You want egg salad sand r P.B. and J.?"

"Let's eat e cherries," Anthony said, smiling, "then Marcos and I can spit pits at each other."

"Oh don't worry about him. He'll get over it. Did I tell you already? Your mother called. She wants to come up for a visit. Honey, I know she'll only stay a few days, but I can't eat all that fried food she makes. I get sick. I don't know how to tell her."

"Where's Annie?" he asked, scanning the beach.

"She went swimming. Take your sandwich, Kyle. She came and told me like you told her to. I saw her a few minutes ago. Anyway, maybe you can tell your mother."

But he wasn't listening. He was searching the bobbing heads in the roped-off swimming area for the one he would recognize as his tow-headed Annie. Seeing that she wasn't among those in the shallows, he focused farther out, near the float. That's where she would be. Annie loved to swim, paddled around 'til her lips were blue and her throat sore.

"Anthony?"

"I don't see her, Lynette," he said, walking now toward the water and the shrieking children. Their splashing slid down the air, which hardened in the light 'til it looked like a pane of glass. By the time he reached the water's edge, he saw Annie, or somehow he was sure it was her, outside the confines of the swimming area, way beyond the float line and getting smaller by the second.

"Jesus, Lynette," he said, though she could not hear him.

The lifeguards had seen Annie now as well, and he ran to where they stood.

"No, don't go in. We don't want to have to haul both of you out of the riptide. Here." The one wearing Ray Bans and a red visor handed him the binoculars, and the other, the barrel-chested one with red fur on his back, dove through the waves.

Anthony put the binoculars to his face, searching for Annie and the telltale arc of the tide, but his eyes were too full of water and when he tried to focus he saw instead his first wife in a sea of blood, the way he'd found her on the tile floor, her hair floating, her wrist open, but no breath in her. And then for no reason he could think of, he was babbling about the shark . . . Marcos' shark. Even as he heard himself repeat it, "His shark is out there!" he knew how inane it sounded.

"Take it easy, man," said the lifeguard, "we pull people out of rips all the time."

He waved his arms helplessly on the beach, hoping she would spot him. The lifeguard ducked a breaker and came up powerfully through the next. He wondered then why he'd run to them, why he hadn't gone straight into the water himself, why he'd spanked Annie the night before, and not Lynette's boys. She ran to her bed to get away from him, and raged as he sat at her side: "It was their idea. Not mine!"

It had started with that stupid board game, Operation, the funny man full of plastic bones and rubber bands. But the wire to the tongs was broken and it wasn't fun anymore because the buzzer didn't go off. So they used the tongs to take Monopoly houses and plastic bones from her underpants. And then it was fingers, Marcos' fingers, peeling her back to look inside. That's how he found them.

"I wanted them to like me," Annie wailed.

And he'd had to explain that those places were private, that men and women used them to love with, that that could be a wonderful thing, but not until children were grown up.

"I want my mother," Annie sobbed.

He took her in his arms then, "I want her too, Annie, but she's gone." And he rocked them both.

The lifeguard was out beyond the breakers, closing in. Did Annie know by now that her legs going round could do nothing against the tide but keep her afloat? "Keep swimming, Annie," he said, "keep swimming."

He took the binoculars again—the lifeguard was now no more than an arm's length from Annie—and his heart sickened as he watched her turn and swim toward the empty horizon.

"What the hell is she swimming away from him for?" shouted the other guard, snatching the binoculars back. And then, raising a fist in the air: "He's got her!"

Anthony felt Lynette behind him, felt her touch on his shoulder, but he could not move.

"I'm sorry," she said.

He heard the tremble in her voice. He felt her need. "Me

too," he said, though he wasn't sure why or for what. He breathed heavily, but did not look at her. Annie was hanging onto the lifeguard's neck, but kicking on her own, swimming back to him. He felt his new wife's eyes bore into his back, and he knew his inability to turn to her might destroy them. The lifeguard was in the shallows now, where he swung Annie from his shoulders in one easy motion and set her on her feet. A moment passed before Anthony recognized the woman who had stepped in front of him and into the water, arms out to Annie.

Moonstone

The realtors call the hills golden. I say the hills are brown. If it gets hotter, they will burn and later look like mangy hide. In the thick air and glint bright light, they shudder . . . poor creatures taking shallow breaths.

I stand at the back door and wave at my husband, then I go inside to write a letter to my lover, Evan. One of my eyes is hooded, the other longer and wide. I have two faces when I say goodbye to Corty at the back door, the dark and the light . . . the weak and the strong if you like. Nothing comes of the transaction. This is the child he has taken in. Two-faced. There isn't one that I trust.

I try not to remember my childhood. No, I wasn't sent to the cellar. There simply was no thread through; there were too many introductions. I couldn't locate my mother's charge account at the hardware, already there were three married names, and she'd gone back to her maiden name in between. By the time my father was done marrying, I was done explaining. The day we did a population study for a sociology class in high school, I could have stood in all four corners of the room. I make up terms now, and I think former is nicer than ex: ex-wife, ex-step-brother, ex-step-sister-father-mother. That is if you want to keep them in your permanent collection.

I could talk about my "my halfmother," my father's "stepwife." She exists . . . his fourth wife, and they don't live together. I think they are too tired of marriage to divorce. I could talk about my "other mother;" my own mother turned to women after her three strikes you're out. It doesn't help me understand why I got married, a year ago. "Oh, you're newlyweds!" people say. And I've heard myself respond: "Yes, it's our first marriage."

I learned to make a drink from one of my mother's suitors who was sitting across the room. A Salty Dog. I'd like one now but I'll wait an hour. I was eleven and didn't know what *can't* meant. "BULLSHIT!" he roared at me as I wept about the fate of the Indians. I don't cry much now. It makes my blood vessels pop. I think I had seven stepbrothers. One of them got mad that I burned out his water bed vibrator. I ran everything high in those days. One of them tried to seduce me in a pile of coats. I smelled Rive Gauche, Norel, and Nina Ricci—dark chocolate and tobacco. I dream about piles of people writhing, people I knew. Some of that head count is my own doing.

I wanted the baby, but I would have talked to him differently if I'd known whose he was. Not for myself, for his understanding. My sister thought to comfort me. She believes she's psychic; for her, nothing is lost. She said children have told their mothers, "I tried to come to you once but I had to go back and wait." I can't believe that. I want to love a man.

Evan, I mistook your signs, the crumbs, corks and shoelaces you dropped on the forest floor. I thought you emptied your pockets so I would trust you. You emptied them so you could find your way back to your wife. In the hotel room, the underside of your tongue flashed like a silver leaf, and the city in the rain below us shed light like a lotus blossom, opening, opening, opening. I love you forever you said, but you made no place for me. Where was I to stay, in the crook of your knee, the hollow of your armpit? And whose fingers would find me there?

My husband sits over my life like an enormous temple Buddha—calculated waiting. He has his suspicions but he would rather not have them. I don't give mixed signals. I don't wait to be found out, and I don't confess. I tell him nothing. If I can't live with it, I can't do it. So far, I haven't done anything that has prevented me from coming home. I'm the eggshell he keeps floating. There's no poetry to steal from him. He shouts, and I tell him I won't tolerate it. Then he shouts louder. When he goes away, he calls me every night at a certain time, sometimes again later, though I'm not always there. It's a weight I can live with. It's his weight I suspend from, he gives me a radius. I suppose I sound back to him, distorted as a fog horn, though resounding for some time. I try to be like that. It's the best I can do.

I used to get a kind of glee out of other people's accidents. I remember the boy who tried to put his body straight out from under one of those chin-up bars that fix between doorways. The suction gave, and he fell, hitting his head on the floor and his chin with the bar. I laughed to tears in the tension. His mother was livid. I know I wouldn't laugh now. Some decisions I've made have become accidents. Evan, for instance. I'd give my husband hell if he had an affair. There is no such thing as mislaid. Miss Took, I've met her. And, yes, I've been Miss Taken too. But am I Mrs. McDaniels? I go to the mailbox and wonder where my first name went.

I told my husband before we went camping last week. I said I couldn't go hiking and I couldn't swim. I sat still while he fished. The sun reached inside the cracks in the granite. The marmots came out and watched me. Private meanings . . . . Is that lying? I told Corty I'd had a miscarriage. I said the word very carefully for him: mis-carriage. And even slower to myself, I miss what I carried.

I told the people at Planned Parenthood I was going to keep the baby—that was before I found the pay phone in the parking lot. They called it "the fetus." I might have loved Evan, before that phone call, before that click like a door shutting against my ear drum. All along, he thought we were playing a game of Spy. He expected me to be better at putting together the clues. *It happened in the parlor with the revolver . . . . No, it happened in the kitchen with the hatchet* . . . . No, it happened in the parking lot with the pay phone. The doctor I went to a few weeks ago explained the surgical procedure to me. He didn't use the word fetus. He called it "conceptual matter."

I've heard that people who live together and supposedly love each other become telepathic. *Ah honey, I was just thinking of iced tea.* If Corty knew my thoughts, I'd be in a cab right now. It's not that he wouldn't forgive me. He wouldn't recover. I don't tell him and I don't recover what's lost. Seems fair.

That day we stopped by the river, Corty, you fell asleep and I went to get the bag of picnic supplies from the car. I hadn't known I wanted it until I saw it—the axe we'd brought camping, used to cut low dry branches from trees. I saw you in my mind's eye, the shadows of leaves playing across your face. I saw that I would cleave your head open from the back so that afterwards I could sit in front of you and pretend it hadn't happened. But beneath your skull, I wouldn't find what it was that I wanted, just more muck and mush the same as that part of you I'd had removed while the machine gasped for air. I'd expected something else. Maybe a moonstone with a clear vein disappearing at its misty center, maybe a soft gray pod with a little sing-song inside— something I could keep anyway, and look at, and say, this was.

Evan should have called me yesterday. He knew when I was coming back from camping. I got ready to see him. I burned my ear on the core of an electric curler. Then I dumped the whole set in the sink and turned the water on, steamed up the mirror so I wouldn't see my red shrieking face.

At night, I dream about his children. I rescue them. I find them lost on a highway in a flat landscape, shifting shades of gray, deserted factories to the east and to the west a churned up sea that washes over the road in places. The wheels begin to slide and I have to keep steering. Even when there is no traction, I have to keep steering.

You . . . *cream butt, mushroom tip, dark curls, darling* . . . . I cannot write you a letter. I cannot bear the humiliation . . . more need and no answer. If I get angrier, I'm not sure that I won't kill you. I know now that I have the capacity to kill.

I get up from the typewriter and go into the kitchen where I make orange spice tea with honey. Then I pour so much brandy in it, the honey won't melt off the spoon. I will write you the letter I wish I'd received. I will write a letter from you to myself. We were close enough that I could do that, exchange myself for you. You were more prudent. Have your caution and your pining then. Me, I hang onto my anger like it was a guard rail in a whirly-gig seat, lest I fly out and hit the hardness of your decision. I deserved better. I will give myself what I deserved. I tried to get the truth from you, and I must have looked like a fool, like a child blindfolded swinging at the air while you yanked the pinata up and down. I don't know what you deserve. Maybe your wife will open the letter.

Dear Madelaine,
It was easier to assume that you understood how things stood between us than to tell you, than to risk losing any of the time I might have had with you. I see that now. For me, ours was a doomed course, but for you, Madelaine, there were no parameters. I told you I didn't know if I loved my wife. That was true. But she and I have a history of love, and for a man my age maybe that is almost as good, better anyway than finding out I can't replace it. You fell in love with the artist in me, and I fell in love with the man you resuscitated. There was no material out of which we could not create each other. We sculpted crone noses and gargoyle grins with leftover mashed potatoes. We illustrated bestiaries of winged and horned creatures jumping from trees. You belly danced in a bed spread, and when you laughed, there was nothing else for me.
I loved you then but I never saw it as a solution. I knew it couldn't keep us aloft forever, hovering above mundane hours, above worry and maintenance. We went on "meeting each other places," but there was to be no homecoming. I'd like to say that I knew that too, when in reality, it was something I decided. I'm sorry about the baby, but the three children I clothe and care for already have reduced me to a signature. I can't afford to create . . . I don't experiment . . . I paint what sells and wait for the checks. Fall in love with your own artist, Madelaine, and cherish the husband that takes care of you.
                                        As ever,
                                          Evan

When I've finished, I seal it in an envelope, put a stamp on it and walk across the street to the mailbox. Tomorrow at this time, it will come back, and I will write in indelible ink marker, NO SUCH PERSON, RETURN TO SENDER.

The sky outside is granular, too blue, like undried paint. I change into my swimsuit and head for the pool. The Yucca stalks clash in combat. Staves pierce the blue and their seeds crawl along my arm hairs. I curl my toes on the rough terra cotta edge of the pool and lean out over my shadow. "Bird of prey," I whisper, "sink her." Then I dive.

I stretch out on my towel. At first I think it is those damn seeds again, hairy little burrs crawling up my legs, but it's not. It's a quiver beneath my skin. I turn my head and find the eyes I feel on me. One of the condominium landscapers is sitting in the truck outside the pool fence. The roof of his mouth is too jammed up with sandwich for him to smile, but he jerks his head, acknowledges that I have seen him.

I smile and turn away. Then I cross my legs so my calves won't bulge against the pavement. I lengthen my neck and pull my shoulder blades back. My chest opens to the sky. My breasts widen and settle against my rib cage. My waist grows long and thin. Let him look.

I wake with a shadow across my face and scramble my belongings together. Corty will be home soon, and I have an urge to go to my studio and make a quick mess, as evidence of a creative day. He works hard with all those people who ride the elevator down on Fridays saying, "Well, it's the weekend. Have a good one," and on Monday go back up asking, "How was your weekend?" and by Wednesday are saying, "It's almost over." Everything almost over—the weekend, the week, week after week.

If I've created something while he was away, he feels it was all worthwhile. I always see it in his face. I come up behind his chair when he's watching sports, and he lets the weight of his head rest against my bosom while I smooth the wrinkles out of his forehead and press my thumb between his eyes. Then I go and make dinner.

On the way in the door, a piece of paper falls from between the pages of my paperback. I close the door with my heel and open it. It reads:

You're quite an attractive woman! I couldn't help but notice! I'm the guy in the truck outside the gate. If you ever want to have a couple of hours of fun without all the bull-shit of relationships, call me at 934-2218, or come by 305 Beechwood. I'm 6'2",185 lbs., 24 years old and single.

Signed,

Bruce Brewster

I put the note under my book on the kitchen table and go get dressed for Corty, who comes in right on time, huge in the doorway and still steaming from several sets of racquet ball.

"How are you? honey."

How am I, honey? I hug and kiss him and notice he looks me over rather carefully. I tell him I still have cramps. I tell him I'm still tired. He suggests the new Chinese place over by the Dry Cleaner. Then I tell him I'm upset.

"By what? sweetheart."

I tell him something happened that upset me, and I hand him the note. His face goes red and he drops his gym bag in the corner. He wants to know how hungry I am. I'm too upset to be real hungry.

"Well, I'm going out then."

I look at the note between his stubby fingers. "Why?" I want to know.

"I'm going to show this guy a couple of hours of fun without all the bullshit of relationships."

I laugh. "Honey, I don't think he could stand more than ten minutes."

My husband grins, and the door slams. I sit at the kitchen table and doodle on a scrap of paper. The doodle looks like blood under a microscope, like blood trying to coagulate. I run to the back door shouting "Come back!" even though I know: there is no coming back.

One of Me Watching

I awakened on the train somewhere between Amsterdam and Copenhagen feeling sunken into myself like a fallen cake. It was the summer I met the Swedish family my mother had married us into. I took the ferry from Copenhagen to Malmo, the southern tip of Sweden, where I was picked up by my eldest cousin who drove me to the summer house in the archipelago. He played the music very loud—the volume up so high, I couldn't even hear the wind. A new English rock band, he told me. It sounded to me like ten people beating their forks on their dinner plates and chanting the menu.

Driving through a field of raps in bloom was like staring into the sun—yellow until the very lines of your iris felt like splinters of light around a gaping hole. For relief, I looked across the North Sea at the heavy clouds that brooded over Denmark and the hard slate color of the water. Everything seemed brilliant or hard.

Lillasundholmen, island in the little straits, it's where I arrived. My mother and Kjell, her new husband, were staying on his boat next to the dock. Above it on a hill sat the big house beneath the birch trees. Like the other buildings on the island, the house was a burnished red, its paint a by-product of a method of copper mining long gone. The property was bordered by a small fjord, beyond it the forest full of sounds feathery and hissing.

I was reading on deck, waiting for the rest of the family to come down for the day's sailing excursion—lying on my stomach because I couldn't get used to the idea of these new relatives seeing me without my top on. I couldn't get used to the idea of having breasts at all. Every time I looked down, I noticed the space between them.

I made my palms into fists and stacked them one on top of the other, resting my chin in the cavity. From this vantage point, I could see everyone on shore whose names I didn't remember yet. My two uncles were inspecting the broken rigging of one of the children's boats. My aunts sat together on the steps of the cabin by the shore, stripping dill, topping beets, and talking. Over the side of the bow, I could see my cousins as they plummeted down into the clear water.

I got up and went to sit above the galley doorway, hanging my feet down over it. "Hand me my T-shirt," I said to my mother who was fixing coffee in the cabin.

"Hasn't anyone ever told you that it's not polite to hang your feet from the kitchen ceiling?" she said, grabbing hold of my swinging legs by the ankles.

"So what," I said, "Nobody cares if you eat naked here either."

I looked at Kjell sleeping. Beneath his mustache, his mouth was small and pursed like a kitten's—fine tilting lines at either side. My mother was watching him too. She stroked her cheek with the tail of her thick braid. It was a signal I knew; Kjell must have been a good lover. I looked at his feet—narrow and bony and in no way warped.

"Kjell has sweet feet," I said to my mother. She came up from the galley, slapping my calves as she emerged.

"You like him better now, don't you?"

"I always did like him," I said, which was true. She stood below me, leaning over the hatch and resting her crossed arms on my knees. I tucked a stray hair behind her ear.

"You don't think I'd do wrong by you, do you?" she asked.

"You left Daddy," I said and shrugged.

"Yes, I did. I left him and he dove to the bottom of a scotch bottle, which is where he was headed anyway. All my fault, huh?"

"I didn't say that," I told her ruefully, wishing I could back-pedal my way out of what I'd started.

"It's not always what people say, you know. No one ever says a bad word about your father. It's because he has a mean streak a mile wide." With that, she pressed my legs and stood back.

"Maybe that's where I got it," I said.

She gave me her hawk-like scanning look. "Maybe," she said, going down into the galley.

Back on shore, my grandfather and Anders were making their way down to the dock. Moggen's body frame was massive, and I saw in his careful determined movements a latent power. I'm sure he would have liked to pick his disabled brother up, carry him under one arm and the ambulator under the other. I jumped down from my perch and stuck my head in the galley.

"I'm sorry, Mother," I said.

"It's all right Frances," she said wearily, and I felt that I had spoiled her mood.

"Did I wreck everything?" I asked.

She came up the stair level with me, and gently put her fist to my cheek. "If it were that easy to wreck my everything, then it wasn't much to begin with. No, baby, you didn't."

"Moggens and Anders are coming now," I said.

"Well good," she said, "then we'll only have to wait another half century."

We stood very close without touching and listened to the halyards ring out against the mast. I took the tail of her braid and wrapped it around my thumb. We were both looking at Kjell, asleep in the sun.

"Watch this," my mother whispered. "Kjell," she said in her melodic voice. He smiled a little but did not wake.

"Do it again," I said.

"Kjell," my mother repeated even more softly—and again the gentle smile. She sighed. "I hate to wake him."

"KJELL!" I shouted. He sat straight up and fixed us with his granite gray eyes.

"You rat," my mother said laughing, and then to Kjell in her most soothing tones, "We thought you'd like coffee."

"You see," I said, turning to follow her, "he doesn't love *me*."

On Kjell's forty-fifth birthday, an hour before we were due at the party, I sat with my mother on the pier, my back against her knees. As we discussed what I would wear, she braided my hair, gathering the stray strands with soft strokes while keeping the plait between the thumb and forefinger of her other hand. I felt the reflection of the sun on the water in the flush of my face and watched the light in the reeds as it shifted between the ridged blades. My mother was talking and I dozed, my eyelashes dividing the fjord in bands of shadow.

"I couldn't ever have afforded to send you to art school at home, or to graduate school for that matter, if you decide later that's what you want. Of course you'll have to start the government Swedish classes soon, but that won't be a problem for you."

My mother liked to believe in me. I was her vehicle of faith. "You can do anything, Frances," she often told me, "anything at all," as though she hadn't had the same option. If I were to have said that she made some choices along the way, she would have reminded me of the letters that supposedly came every Christmas from my father's lawyer, threatening to take her to court, threatening to take me away; and it was this she told me that kept her from going back to school, that kept her at the job she didn't like. I don't remember my parent's divorce, and I never saw the letters.

According to my mother, there were no limitations on my happiness. I could get my Ph.D. if I wanted, become a brilliant professor or museum curator or psychiatrist—all the things she thought she might have been good at. And then I could glow in the knowledge of having rectified her mistakes. My mother picked men like dandelions and blew the hot rage of her unsatisfied wishes on them until they scattered like seed.

The party in celebration of Kjell's forty-fifth birthday was at Krista and Murre's house across the fjord. Kjell's childhood friends came around the house to the backyard where the tables had been set beneath the trees. They came carrying between them a string of candy and singing.

I ended up in the kitchen with Krista and Murre where I asked Murre what he did, and he told me that he sold castors for office furniture. "The little metal balls," he said, making a circle with thumb and forefinger, shrugging and smiling as if to imply that he'd long ago accepted that there wasn't much to say about it. He fished a cigar out of his pocket, poked it playfully at Krista's ribs and left the clamor of the women who were assembling in the kitchen.

Krista gave me some cucumbers to peel, and after making a sound of annoyance in her throat, explained to me in English, "He smokes cigars all day. In the morning, he spits in the sink, doesn't bother to wash it away." She poured a heavy cream over a casserole of fish in a glass pan and as we watched the cream rise over the shiny filets, she continued to vent her outrage. "He wears a gun around the house sometimes too, thinks he is John Wayne, the barrel shoved in the waistband of his pants, my God!"

To me, Murre looked as though he might have been as tall as his wife when he was twenty-two, but years of telephone sales had caused his spine to sink. The roll around his midriff was such that standing up, he couldn't possibly have pressed his groin against her. I saw that when he came in and kissed her, a smooch so loud I knew it must have been for my benefit. Krista had a loose eye, like a fish in a round bowl, magnified and looming one instant, the next sliding away. I finished peeling the cucumbers but left them uncut by the sink.

I didn't see anywhere to sit in the living room so I stood by the door. My great-uncle, Anders, was the only other person standing, leaning against the far wall by the dining room table. His face had the look of a jack-o'-lantern abandoned on the back porch, smiling crookedly into a swirl of leaves, and slumping further. His eyes too, it seemed, bore the weight of rotten pulp, though it was booze and cigarettes that had swelled his lids so that they hung down into his field of vision. And no one in the family was quite sure what Anders' field of vision included. My grandfather, Moggens, had explained to me that when Anders looked at your face, he saw only your shoulders, but that when he looked above your head, he saw your head. I had gotten used to him staring at the air above my head. From the change in his expressions when we talked, I knew that was where he saw my face.

The faces of Kjell's friends were marked by weariness, not striving—good faces all the same. His friends were people who had made themselves content with what they had found, who hadn't gone far looking for it. They asked about Kjell's travels, becoming both intimidated and jealous, and marveled at how he had retained his youthful looks. "People who keep the world running," my mother said of his friends, "the ones we should be grateful to for keeping home the same." I didn't know what she could have meant by that for us, considering the number of places we'd lived, but my grandparents still lived in the house where she was born, and I almost could have found their faces at that party, if I'd looked.

My mother was waving to me across the room and I headed dutifully in her direction, steeling myself for another round of introductions. Everyone kept telling me how lucky I was, as though I'd been waiting my whole life to become Kjell's stepdaughter. They didn't know what else to say. They wanted to see if I was nice, and they hoped Kjell wasn't unlucky for having gotten a package deal. I was very nice. It didn't mean anything. Social pleasantries are like worry beads: everyone fidgeting with them incessantly, clacking them together.

I drifted into the dining room where a group of men were sitting at the table discussing the economy or cars; I couldn't tell which because the only words I recognized were Volvo, Saab, and *huit*, the latter being the Swedish word for shit, close in sound to its English counterpart and said with the same vehemence. I looked at my grandfather's cigarettes on the table. I knew I should stop stealing from him and just ask for one in private.

I liked going to find Moggens, alone in his study. As we talked, he'd rub his eye with his thumb while holding a cigarette between his first two fingers, from time to time singeing his forelock but too intent on the conversation to be much troubled by it. He was the one I knew to ask for Anders' story, the one who told me that Marthe was the name of Anders' wife—headstrong, young Marthe who took her daughter to swim in the rough waters on the west coast. Anders tried to rescue them, one under each arm, then one lost—Anders not knowing which it was. That's when his head met the rock and his wife went to sea. That's how he got the brain hemorrhage.

Moggens caught my questioning glance (I was trying to figure out how to make off with one of his cigarettes), and mistook it for curiosity. The men at the table were still laughing over a joke he'd just finished. "Come over here," he called, "come over and I'll tell you."

"Yes," my Uncle Hasse said, wiping his eyes, "tell her the King of the Shit House story."

"Ah, now you've ruined it," Moggens exclaimed, dropping both hands to the table.

"No, he hasn't," I insisted, "tell me." I leaned against Moggen's chair and he put his arms around my hips.

"Well, once there was a maintenance man for apartment buildings, and as extra work on holidays—you understand this man worked all the time—he worked at the train station bathroom. This fellow, he was a very straight fellow, never let bums loiter or slide down walls, never was afraid to approach drunks or toughs, never even considered being afraid . . ."

"And me," my uncle interjected, hitting himself in the chest with his thumb, "I become a professional so the government can take eighty percent."

My grandfather put up his hand at which Hasse downed his schnaps and grunted.

"So one day the railway station manager approached this man because he'd heard that the government was accepting bids on the leasing of the bathrooms. 'No' the man said, 'they would never choose me,' but his wife, she forces him to put in a bid, and he gets it. So now he makes . . . oh, 200,000 kroner a year in black money."

"Who can count the coins for the toilet!" my uncle roared.

"And," Moggens continued, "he is by our standards a millionaire. In the United States, you have movie stars. In Sweden, the King of the Shit House gets rich!"

At this, the men chuckled, except of course my uncle who was rapping his knuckles on the table. I smiled and squeezed Moggens' shoulder, but I had only been half-listening, the rest of my attention on Anders who stood against the wall on the other side of the room.

While Moggens had been telling his story, Anders' mouth had been working, forming words he couldn't get out. I moved to him, leaned over his ambulator and ran my hand across his forehead, pressing down the veins that had risen there. He closed his mouth, and as he smiled his eyelids drooped with the release of the strain.

The men at the table resumed their discussion. I heard the word Electrolux mentioned several times. Anders seemed to be listening, though he stared steadily at me. He curled his fingers and very deliberately made a tunnel of his hand. When he was sure my attention was fixed on it, he dropped his hand to his crotch and made a loud, wet, sucking sound, saying quite clearly and with exaggerated satisfaction: "Electrolux . . . my first woman." The moment after he said it, he shook his head as if to deny it, and then he grinned. I laughed so hard with him it made me weak, and I hung on to the other side of his ambulator until I felt my mother's eyes on me.

That night at the dinner table, I chose to sit next to Anders; he was the only person I could supply with words. He would lose words he wanted and become reconnected to others he didn't want.

"I want the tomatoes," he said. So I passed him the tomatoes. He shook his head. "I want," he paused, "the tomato." I took the spoon, believing that he wanted a slice of tomato, and served him. He slumped further into his chair and began again. "I want," he said, and pointed, I thought, at the fruit basket.

"Ah," I said, "the fruit." He was still pointing so I took an apple and a banana from the basket. He took the apple from my hand.

"An apple," he said slowly, marveling at its shape and the feel of the word on his tongue. Then nodding at me in encouragement, he spoke in Swedish and waited for my response.

So I repeated the words to him, making my best effort at pronunciation. "*Jag har ett apple och en banan.*"

"Jah," he said with the sharp intake of breath particular to Swedish inflection.

"Jah," I answered, and in the end we both considered that we had done rather well.

By early evening, the party had moved to the backyard where the children were playing soccer. I saw my mother at the water pump and noticed how pretty she'd become since we'd moved to Sweden. She was wearing one of Kjell's shirts, the tail of it outlining her ample rump rather nicely. Kjell was often patting her there, when she leaned over to peer into the oven or to spit toothpaste into the sink. He wasn't a rump slapper like her last boyfriend, and I didn't think I'd ever wake to find him breathing over my bed. Now we called her last boyfriend "bog breath" and "mouth breather," when we mentioned him at all.

Krista and Murre were out on the driveway. He'd come back from making a run to the store for sugar, and she'd been clipping flowers. She stood by the car, one arm dangling with the weight of the shears. He hung his arms over the open door and his bad air blew into her wispy hair. From the look on his face, she'd just told him that in all the time they'd known each other, he'd been rubbing her clitoris backwards. She strode off, carrying the flowers, blooms down, in a stranglehold. He slammed the door, eyeing the men in the yard with the bottle between them, wondering how in hell you figure out what is frontwards and backwards of a thing not shaped for travel anyway, bow and stern, yes. Yes, I'm sure he suddenly yearned to be out on his boat, which unlike his wife would signal the first moment of miscalculation. And me, I yearned to be away from all these people—away where my imagination would not have the chance to give meaning to conversations I scarcely understood a word of.

I walked quickly into the forest at the edge of the garden. Birch, aspen, oak, and spruce vied to turn their leaves in the sun, to display their own variant of green, and the forest floor was laced with leaves like interlocking fingers. The sun was slinking behind a veil of cloud. In the sudden damp of the woods, I felt stricken at having left my mother alone back there. But it crossed my mind then too, that it was me that felt alone in the midst of my new family, not her.

I remembered the day before my mother left for Sweden, and I for my grandparents'. We stayed in bed all morning, reading magazines, letting the phone ring, filling out a computer dating application together. I read aloud to her: "If none of the answers following a particular question is the exact answer you wish to give, then mark the answer that comes closest." The vase of flowers I'd put on her breakfast tray fell over, and when finally she stopped laughing, she told me it was true—that most of her friends had given up on finding the *right* man and picked the man that came closest. The friends that kept looking also kept marrying. I asked her if that was true of her, and she winced, as though I had made a loud noise or pulled the shade up.

"Maybe," she said, "but that's over now."

The application listed thinking as an activity right along with hiking, sailing and skiing. I told her I would check only that box. I said it to cheer her up, but I would have done just that, and waited to see who I got. It was the closest I could come to a mystery box.

Once out of the forest, I walked along a path through the marsh grass until I came to a beach where I saw a row of bathhouses, all of them boarded up. I knocked at the first one anyway and saw myself as in a dream: one of me watching, one of me doing. The other of me stepped lightly from the bathhouse in a black knee-length bathing suit with bloomers, and a silk bathing cap adorned with a pink rosette.

"And who will go for a swim with me?" she shouted, and when she saw that the beach was empty, she disappeared.

I knocked at the next bathhouse and saw the door fly open so forcibly it banged against the side of the building, and myself in seven layers of raw linen and a waistband of gold and serpentine, my hair bound by a sinew of green willow.

"Where is his ship?" she shouted, and when she saw that the sea was empty, she disappeared.

I didn't bother to knock at the next bathhouse, and the only version of me that wouldn't disappear ground a deep pivot in the sand with her heel and headed for the stretch of beach where all sign of humanity had long since been erased by pattern of wind and wave. I was drawing on the air with the tip of a feather when I saw a bolt of silver break the water and Anders emerge, shedding light droplets from his shoulders, opening his fingers skyward. Young, lean, smiling at me, he dove. And I waited. I waited for the longest time. Then I walked till I imagined I was just a speck of the girl that had started off.

All the phrases in Swedish that I no longer wanted in my head and which were never there when I needed them kept busting in on my thoughts. *Nei tac, jog har en kupp kaffe just innen jog komma hite. No thank you, I had a cup of coffee just before I came here.* I said the phrases aloud and after awhile was rid of them, content to concentrate on the hum of the wind against the white feather in my hand.

Kjell was nearly abreast of me before I heard the soles of his feet squeak against the sand. He was red in the face from exertion, and his eyes radiated such fierce concern, I couldn't look at him. It was as though I'd never seen him before, as though he'd been a rock to me, and I'd thought to myself whenever I saw him: that rock is boring black and white. But then the sun had emerged from behind a cloud and picked up all the tiny particles of mica in the stone and thrown their light like glitter in the air.

I stared at our bare feet in the sand, both of us making furrows with our toes. I stared at our feet hard, in expectation, hoping to find clues in the conversation our toes were having for the one we should start.

When finally Kjell had gotten his breath, he asked, "Are you all right, Frances? Why did you leave?"

I looked up at him then and felt something hideous rising from the bottom of my stomach, some gargantuan beast about to crash and heave through the underbrush. "I hate your friends!" I shouted.

He let me breathe awhile after that. I had to. The tears that came to my eyes flowed fast and freely no matter how I mopped at them with the cuff of my sweater. He reached out to touch my face but I pulled away.

"Let's walk," he said quietly, turning towards the house.

We both looked at the water, listening to the gentle over-lap of waves and the accompanying motif our footfalls made.

"I'm sorry," I said at last.

He shrugged, appearing aggravated, and said, "You don't have to be. I've known them all forever, and I've hated each and every one of them at a different time."

I looked at him, incredulous.

"No, it's true," he said, looking away. "I went to Tunisia once with Jonas and Birgitta, on vacation, except there was a flood, and the two of them, Jesus, they sat around in the hotel room drinking all day and sulking like babies. And Roger, he got fat since I went to the States, and turned chicken shit, sold his sailboat for a motor boat. And Krista, what a case, seeing a psychiatrist three times a week, all the time telling everybody she wants to divorce Murre but she's too afraid. Then when they go on vacation, she threatens to jump overboard and kill herself."

"You're kidding."

"No, I'm not," he said, "and I could tell you worse."

"Well then who do you like?" I blurted out.

We stopped before the dark tunnel of trees that led back to the house, and when he turned his eyes towards me, I was stunned again by their brilliance, but I didn't look away.

"Like," he said slowly, contemplating the meaning of the word. "No one, but your mother I love, and love is all the time, then the rest doesn't matter so much."

Lena, my grandmother, said Anders couldn't walk with-out the four-pronged ambulator, but I found out it wasn't true. One morning, I woke at three and saw the sun rising, trailing yellow streamers all across the sky. I knew it would stay that way for hours, that I could turn my back on the moment I longed to savor, and when I turned round again, it would still be there—the light just the same. I went down-stairs to the front room with its big windows. The ducks were barking the way they do with too much water in their gullets. Then I heard Anders' door open and the terrible crashing that followed.

Before he could get a foot in front of him, his upper body fell forward. At that moment, he slammed a hand flat on the wall and with the retrograde motion, threw one of his legs out. Although older than Moggens, he had no fear of brittle bones. He wrapped his arms around corners and reached for walls as though they were rings to swing by.

When finally he saw me sitting on the couch, he smiled his side-sagging smile, and leaning over his left foot, he took a huge step with his right. His gait was like that of a child at the age when walking is a precarious gathering of momentum. Watching him, I felt the earth did not go round evenly at all.

I got up and took his arm, and using me instead of the walls to swing towards and away from, he made his way to the couch. We sat and watched the low hummocks of islands come up off the flat horizon as the sun struck them. We watched the light running down the filament of the fish nets stretched out on the rack beside the docks; the air itself like them, full of light droplets running down trajectories. Very suddenly, he touched my cheek.

"Marthe," he said softly.

Without thinking, I answered, "No, I'm not Marthe, I'm Frances," and then I saw him wince. And then I knew it wasn't simply a word he'd lost.

During Kräfskiva, the feast in celebration of the early fall and the coming of the small, red crawdads, I sucked dill butter and brine from between spiny legs before cracking open the kräfta with my thumbs. Red was the color of the season: bright change against new cold. The ronne berries on the window sill were the same color as the crawfish we ate, as the lady bugs I shook off the quilt before bringing it in from the line, as the cherry juice on my mother's lips. We picked the last of the cherries together in the orchard behind the house.

"Imagine," my mother said, "the people who lived here made everything, from the garden to the fish nets. And now we're so worried about becoming specialists."

"Mom, the pioneers did everything too" I reminded her.

"Exactly," she said, smiling gaily, the basket of cherries

balanced in the crook of her arm. She had a way of assuming anything I said to the favor of her argument—that it might have been a challenge didn't occur to her. I kept wondering how I could be so hateful. 'Look,' I wanted to say, 'it's not all that unique here.' But I knew what she would say, and I knew it was no alternative. So did she, which is why she would have told me, "You can go live with your father if you don't like life with me."

I didn't push it because I didn't want to hear that ultimatum again, and I didn't want to be fixing Bloody Marys for my father on Sunday mornings. Besides, I was just thinking how much I was getting to like my room with its wallpaper of blue corn flowers and the wood burning stove and the fir bench with a straight back like a church pew and the foot pedal organ—even how much I was beginning to like Kjell and the smell of fresh wood shavings in his mustache when he kissed me good morning.

Back in the kitchen, I watched the cherries tumble from my mother's basket into the colander. She handled them with care, and they glistened in the water like dark rubies. My grandmother was sifting flour for a cake while outside Kjell made a saw sing across the boards he'd measured to fix the roof. He came in to drink and stopped for a moment behind my mother. He dangled a cherry by its stem above her head, like a lure on a line, and she went up on her toes after it. I could hear them laughing as I snuck up the stairs to my grandparents' quarters.

My new grandmother was demented about her dogs—pictures of her two dachshunds right up there on the wall alongside her real grandchildren, both dogs with that stricken look common to most non-poisonous bat-boned creatures. And Lena was kind. At each new moon, she bent her knees three times and made a wish. And all the wishes she made were for the protection of her loved ones. Still, she was not as honest as my grandfather. I'm sure it was she who sorted through the box of photographs brought to me and my mother; she, who removed Kjell's first wife from the family reunions, looking at each photo before she tucked them away somewhere. But upstairs, that afternoon, I found the one I was looking for, the one that slipped through because it was of thinner paper and had been cut with nail scissors into a heart shape. The wife was just the way I wanted her to be—thin and dark, a real sulky beauty—nothing like my mother.

Moggens didn't purposely leave the "just married" photo of Kjell and his first wife out on his desk in the study. From the tarnish on the silver frame, I judged he'd never moved it since he set it there. Kjell's older face was more likeable, craggy and a bit ruined.

Back in the kitchen, my aunts clucked their tongues about Anders. It made Kjell fume. He told me that when they were children, he would row across the fjord while his sisters washed rocks with their tooth brushes. "Nothing is changed," he said.

My aunts told me that Anders used to have a meticulous and conscientious nature. They said that he was good with the children, that he could run a relay with an egg on a spoon clamped in his mouth, and never once lose the egg. They thought it was a shame what the change had brought: how he put his cigarettes out in his coffee cup, and used slang, and swore too much. "I want to piss," he'd say in the middle of dinner.

For two days, he'd complained of a crick in his back. My aunts humored him, and Lena told my grandfather to turn Anders' mattress, which he dutifully went and did. But in the kitchen Anders started up again.

"Damn," he stuttered, "damn," until finally my grandmother said to him:

"Damn crick in your back. That's right Anders. Always something there is with you, always something there will be with you."

After she left the room, he made a fist and swung at the air, so sharply I heard his arm lock in the socket. Then he said very clearly to me, "There, the crick is gone."

"Someone is missing," my grandfather said as he took his place at the table laden with steaming crawfish and bottles of schnaps. "Ah, there she is, my wife." He made a toast and everyone looked around the table before they drank.

I'd been seated at the far end away from Anders, who stared glumly at his plate, which had been piled with food, precluding the interruption of his requests. I held Moggens' hand while he repeated a joke slowly for my benefit. His calluses felt like the ridges of a dried corn husk. I lost the gist of the joke. It seemed that I had been wandering around for days behind people, not knowing where I was going until we arrived. For days repeating words in Swedish after my grandmother—the words for electric stove, can opener, frying pan—none of them could I remember. I longed to lean my head against Moggens' chest so that I could hear the tones of his voice and cease to impute sense to the words. I didn't get the punchline of the joke, but when everyone laughed, I laughed too, laughed until my face felt like a mask I wanted to hold at arm's length and shake above the fire.

I left to have dessert with my seven tow-headed cousins at the children's table. They asked me to read the mustard and caviar tubes, and we all laughed at my pronunciation—laughed fit to kill. At least I knew what we were laughing about.

The sound of the sea moving back into a marsh is startlingly loud when you come upon it alone. I looked back towards the house and watched Anders slowly making his way to the center of the yard where the wreath of Midsummer still stood, dry and shaking apart in the wind. I thought of Marthe and how long it had been since anyone mentioned her name.

The children were flying past Anders' legs on an old sled that Kjell had fitted with wheels. They rode the sled in pairs. I reached the top of the hill in time to see another two launched. The boy steered while the girl lay beneath him and screamed.

The wind blew Anders' child-fine tuft of hair to the other side of his head, and he smashed it flat with the palm of his hand. Lena opened the back door and called him in. Ignoring her, Anders gripped the sides of his ambulator and whistled as the children went by. I waved to her and shouted that I would stay with him. Still, she called to him again. He turned and bellowed something ferocious, then thrusting the ambulator ahead of him, he took a few more steps away from the house.

The long branches of the birch trees rose up in an arc and snapped back down with the force of the wind. The sky had grown heavy and thick with clouds. *"Vacket vader vi har iyen,"* I said, smiling at Anders. *What weather we have.* It was a phrase he had taught me the day before. He focused on that place in the air where he saw my face and began.

"I want . . . I want . . . I want to go . . ."

"Where?" I asked cheerfully, supplying him with "to the sauna, to the boat, to the porch." But he didn't begin the teaching game, and the muscles of his face stiffened as he tried again.

Finally he managed: "I want . . . to go . . . fast."

"All right, Anders," I said. "All right, let's go fast for once." I took the rope attached to the sled and moved a little farther up the hill. The children stood back in a semicircle, giggling at the prospect of their great-uncle and me on the sled. I lay down on it first and discovered that the handles also functioned as brakes, having a metal tab which could be brought to bear on the rubber tires.

Anders stood behind the sled and let himself fall forward. I was amazed at the strength of his arms as he caught and held himself above me. Then he covered me with his body, and I watched the tires sink into the ground.

He arched his back and removed my braid from under his chest. For a moment, he held it between thumb and forefinger, feeling the thickness of the plait, moving along it towards the nape of my neck. Then he tucked it gently under my chin, and placed his hands over mine on the controls.

Off we went, the grass occupying nearly the entire foreground of our view—a strip for water, a strip for sky. We hit a bump. The pier seemed to tilt upwards out of the water into the clouds. The boat's mast punctured the sky, and we came to a halt.

The children and I dragged the sled with Anders on it back up the hill. His cheeks were flushed, and the children had him laughing with their exaggeration of the strain. At the top, he refused to get off the sled, saying, "Myself . . . this time alone."

The second time, he went down full speed. I watched him take the jolts of the uneven pier and soar off the end of it still holding onto the controls of the sled. I remember the moment fractured from time, hard as crystal, as though my own stillness could suspend him in the air, but I must have been running. After the splash, at the center of the widening circle of water, I saw Anders' pale hair spread like a dazzling quick bloom, then vanish. I dove for the glimmer of his white shirt and the flash of the sled's silver rail.

My fingers cramped with cold around a mug full of coffee and cognac, I told my new family that I had had Anders' hand in mine—that I'd let go when I could have saved him. The tears dripped from my grandmother's chin onto the table.

"No," Lena said, "he was seeking an oblivion. It was his will, not his weight . . . those useless legs."

Then I remembered clearly and kept quiet. Anders had found my hand in the black water, though it was me that pulled away, for lack of air, yes, but mostly because of the shock of his firm grip. I had tried to shout my name into the water, swallowed the sound of it and choked. I still don't know what made him realize I wasn't Marthe, his wife. But it was he who released me, not the other way around.

The plates in the kitchen were piled next to the sink, crawfish shells scattered along the counter. My grandfather paced between doorways, refilling his cup, leaving the kitchen, returning—stopping to run his hand over the back of my head. The room was humid from our tears and rank with the smell of fish. I got up to wash my face and came upon Kjell and my mother, standing in the foyer hugging.

I turned to walk into the other room, but Kjell had already seen me. He reached out with one arm and called my name, and I moved slowly into the center of their embrace. Before I closed my eyes and let my breath out against my mother's shoulder, I thought of Anders, swimming in the dark current where I hoped he'd find his wife.

Talking a Parrot Out of a Tree

Knowing when to bare your soul and when to bare your teeth, you said that was wisdom. If only I'd kept my clothes on. You were my teacher, my mentor, unsparing and cherishing at the same time. You spent long solicitous afternoons with my poems, you rolled up your shirt sleeves and went at it like work, just plain work, squinting your eyes and sighting down the lines like they were newly planed boards. You were so much older and so married and we were so impossible, it made me feel I had a heart again. I have always been so good at making men fall in love with me, I don't know where or why in me the penchant for it, childhood vengeance of a kind, I suppose. I was always being told to love people, passed like a shuttle from side to side of a loom, a base color to offset the zigzag design of my parents between lovers.

When I was sixteen, a man who was older to me then, though not so old as you are to me now, took me to a nightclub in Zurich. It was summer and I was wearing very thin Indian cotton, and it felt, oh I don't know, soft the way a woman's long hair can feel sliding over your arms. I was very pleased with the outfit, all of one piece, little strings tied at my shoulders in bows, Sultan-style pants gathered at the ankle. I felt someone press a finger into the small of my back, and I turned my head to look over my shoulder. A flower-selling crone, her skin blanched and chalky as stale pasta, raised her bouquet of roses to me in salute, then crooking her finger, she ran her knuckle over the notches in my spine. She wanted me, that I knew, and when she raised her roses again, I reared back, afraid that she would touch me with them like a wand and I would have everything I desired in an instant, and in an instant be dropped to the bottom of her boiling pot. Did I do that to you? Did I? I didn't mean to. Most of life is lived in what we don't mean to do.

I seem to get on better with men, making me, I suppose,

a man's woman, but it's women who don't get on with me, because I love what is beautiful in them, because I would teach them how to have their beauty. I saw my mother wait for virtue, sweeping spiders into dust pans, throwing old spices away, tying ribbons on balloons—earning the right to be noticed, she thought. I broke my plate when I left home. I won't go round feeling like a dry tack biscuit, tamped flat from both sides by a man's toughened palms, waiting for later to be taken out, soaked to life in his saliva.

Making men fall in love with me required only two things: the declaration that I, of course, could never love, because after my unspeakably terrible childhood (and here I swathed myself in a mystery that normality would never have allowed), I could not believe in love; and the confession that I feared madness, that inaccessibility created by my profound disillusion. It saved me from a lot of boring conversation. Other women, more beautiful than I, constant, compassionate and worthy, sat well in their saddles and watched their men chase the one who clung to the mane of her mount, eyes tightly closed. Desperation is so exciting, it promises extremes men can pretend they weren't asking for, all in the name of rescue, and I didn't allow anything to last long enough to become tiresome. It was so easy, it's laughable to me now. All I had to do was speak in half-lines and go barefoot while the others wore shoes.

You weren't the slightest bit interested. Just for once the game couldn't be played, and I was broken of the habit forever. You were so tolerant and tender and sometimes I could hear in your voice that you were dealing with me and I struggled to hear you through the surge and roar of my pride. If my childhood was unhappy, was it not rich and textured and free and was I not loved and warred over with abundant confusion? And the very experiences I thought were lacking, weren't those the ones that others pointed to as the source of their childhood misery? As for madness, you told me you were only interested in functional madness, and get to work. Clearly I was functional, able to see the world through my portal of poetry. But you didn't diminish me by dismissing my sources of power. Like an old warlock musing on the next order of the hour, you had new and more powerful hexes to teach me. We are the dreamers, you told me, struggling to shake ourselves from the night's hold, sliding on daylight into trances, easily able to spend half our lives there. Probably we did in another age, before profit made shame of dreaming.

Under your tutelage, I dethroned the tragedy queen. You said that if I examined every awful thing anyone had ever said about me and allowed it to be true, I'd see that I was no Jezebel, only that I loved truth more than people. Now that you have been in my bed, I think you excuse me too much. I can understand why you said that, but I'm as banal as everyone else wandering around wanting someone to love them. Don't try to make me stronger than you, don't discount comfort. I didn't know that you ever watched me, my lips meeting the edge of the cup, the furious way I cross out words.

This is what I know about myself and people: I want to reach my hands into their bowels and feel their guts pump, I want them to know that every second, every millisecond, every nanosecond is a spurt of change. "Why? why? why?" a child persists in asking. Our veins pump in time to the question.

All attunedness, all attentiveness, all attraction. I don't resist living. Perhaps in another life, I will be more alive than this.

So many people dam up their depths at either end: inlet, outlet. You can see the turbidity in their eyes. Like lakes without flow, pollen settles on the surface, plankton blooms beneath, less and less can they see into themselves, though they try to find more ways to answer the why of everything, the why of anything, hardening their exteriors with repeated reasoning, thickness upon thickness. I have a talent for divination, a passion for finding fault lines, for breaking people open to themselves, a passion that makes my limbs vibrate in my chosen lover's hands like a divining rod while the waters rise to a point closest the surface, and then, unashamed, I will dig like a dog until I have drunk. But I don't love that particular him or another, though I can say I love them all and want none of them and am willing to be sad over it.

Many things feel like they ought to be possible. Flying for instance, and breathing under water. The same with making love to you. You alone knew my work, crafted in contradiction. You understood that I wanted to be more mysterious than the hieroglyphs of a lost language, to have you for my translator, washed with beads of sweat. You, my scholar, burning oil lamps until daylight, measuring my meanings carefully before you poured them into new containers.

I liked the moment that preceded our disaster best. You came to my place, since you were downtown already, and campus was farther for both of us. We sat in the window seat as we did that other time you came over, in the winter when I had had the flu and you came to give me my portion of papers to correct, only this time there was sun on our backs.

Our formality was intact, our pencils sharpened, the coffee service set out. Then you peeled an orange, all in one piece, coaxing the skin from the flesh with gentle pressure, winding the spiral back together and setting the hollow globe in my hands. In that sun filled moment, did the likeness of our minds seize on a symbol to make safe our desire? Stripped down, emptied, made whole again. It doesn't matter now. You placed a section of orange in my mouth, and another in your own mouth, and we sat there with the sun on our backs surprised at how we could look at each other with sweetness flooding our tongues.

I cried afterward, and I still wanted you, even though close up your breath smelled of age, like marsh grass at low tide, the places where ducks wallow, mud stuck with feathers, thick sinking mud. You held my head in your hands, thumbs at my temples. "Your beauty," you said, smiling gently, "has scared this old body of mine silly." But I couldn't stop crying. I cried in the way that children cry who've made themselves ache with want for a thing they've been told already they cannot have, inconsolable until they sleep. "My mistake," you said again and again, rocking us both, and your deep set eyes were vaults of shadow.

I didn't want to add you to the others in my mind, that seemed the worst indignity, the worst that I could do to you. I see now what happened instead; you broke me from the chain. But at the time, I only felt the defeat of our physicality, shame for the bodies that had made us obstacles to each other. My words did not have the power to make you young and desiring. What then were words for?

Trying to sleep next to you, I felt like a child lying in a low-slung hammock, dying to brace its heels against the hemp and lock its knees and pitch all its weight to swinging while the rope groaned slowly, but I feared to, feared the rictus of the rope and the sudden snap and the shudder of my body against hard ground. I stroked your silvery head, watching the twilight come and wondering when your wife Rosie expected you to dinner. You always said those words all together, "my wife Rosie," as though there could be no wife not Rosie, no Rosie not wife.

When I did sleep, the darkness behind my eyes was an expanse of black sand where I lay staked beneath a sun that swung like a pendulum. And I woke ready to beg, yes, ready to beg for your sweat to pour over me, balm to my burn, but when I touched you, you felt dry like a shed skin, slaked off by some living creature.

Endearment took the place of our working formality, that acknowledgement of affection sans sexuality. It was a rough transition, but not a bad trade-off. You held me loosely at the door and I swayed in your arms like wind chimes hitting notes for no one. When you drew away, your eyes were fierce and teary, and I knew you were angry at being old. "There's no need to talk about it now, is there?" you asked.

"And no poems," I answered, before closing the door.

I am going away with a man I met, to the mountains, which is why I called your wife today. I wanted to return the books you loaned me, and tell you myself, and put off having another appointment with you, for now, yes, but possibly forever. It's true, I could have taken them to campus, but I wanted to meet her. You couldn't be for me, but it seemed you held out a promise of what *might* be for me, and I wanted to see what you had.

She was wearing one of your shirts and she was covered in paint and she left a white thumb print on your book though she didn't seem to notice. I never knew gray hair could be so thick and curly; I thought it went gray before it went straight before it fell out. I don't know what I expected her to look like, a faded floral print? She had a face like wide open sky, eyes that could eat up acres. She took me to the basement where she had a bench of woodworking tools, and showed me the table she'd been making look like marble. The sprinklers were running and I could smell something baking in the oven. I got the feeling your whole house is her workshop, that she clears a place for you in it in the evenings.

"He's spoken so highly of your work," she said to me warmly, as though it were better praise to give your praise a second time, and I was touched by the esteem in which she holds you. Clearly without jealousy of me, without need of your praise for her own work.

I looked at the swell of her bosom in your old shirt and imagined her filling up your arms, imagined the two of you together at night. Though your hands haven't worn grooves on each other's bodies, your minds have, and it was effortless—the two of you flowing together from different sources like spring run-off.

She said you were out helping a neighbor find his lost pet, and suggested I wait a bit. "The poet is talking a parrot out of a tree," she said laughing. I imagined the parrot sidling out to the end of a branch towards you, his orange and black eyes spinning like pin wheels. I hoped it would take a long time. I wanted to stand in the kitchen with your wife and lick her mixing spoons and scrape the last batter from the bowl. I wanted to be her initiate, I wanted to learn how to rub color into wood grain, and how to deal with an obstinate child, and how many thorns to count before cutting a rose, and how to make beeswax candles burn longer, and how to stay married to a man maybe a bit like you.

I asked for paper to write you a note, and while she was turning off the sprinklers, I put it in your study. I didn't think she would mind. Your desk was covered with papers and the papers covered with your writing, which looks the way an itch would if you could see it on skin. Your scribble suffers such vertical displacements, it reminds me of a seismographic chart. I realize now there are many trembles and ripples in the ground you walk. My note was absolutely like any other note I have written to you, except that I told you I was going away for awhile and I knew you wouldn't suppose I went alone, and I signed it "with love," which I hadn't ever done before. I didn't mention that I took the small picture of you and your wife and your two daughters, took it right off your desk in the frame and put it in my purse. It was the last thing I did before leaving the room and I didn't stop to ask myself why.

In the front hall, your wife took my hand, as if to shake it, but instead she turned it palm up in her own. She banded my wrist with her thumb and pressed back at my pulse in time to the throb of my blood. "You have a strong heart," she said, stepping back from me. "I know, because I have one too."

"Yes," I said, letting her words steep in silence while I found a commonplace that was safe but true. I wanted to tell her that you had given me back my heart, instead I said, "I'm glad to have met you at last."

"He will always be pleased to hear from you," she said, opening the door for me.

I admired her for that, for not using "we" falsely, for not saying, *do come back and see us*. Perhaps she doesn't know about you and me, but she knows anyway how we've felt. And she knows I love you, and that I'd come to see her.

It won't be easy to go away with someone else. I am afraid to say his name, afraid if I say it I will write it down, submit him to the dangers of my art: losing him in life, gaining him on paper. My poems are never longer than a page. I trace the lines of his palms, wondering if memorizing them might not replace the need for a name. I know I will miss you. I know I will feel like saying to this man, "pull over at the next rest stop and read all of my poetry." Artists are always mooning around over other artists, because their work has no absolute value, because no one can say of it, "See the water coming through that tube, see this cylinder turning, see the electricity flowing through that wire, see it works!"

Interpretation is so personal. People will speculate about your life, disagree with your morality, send your narrators to institutions. I've grappled with my need for you, tackled it with a bone-crunching weight. I've reviewed it in the context of my life as though my life were a manual I could remove from the glove compartment, and flipping to the index, shed some *how-to* on an abstract idea. The index of course is full of musicians and painters and poets, would-be musicians, painters and poets, and the drugs that disconnect people from themselves, that allowed me to find "creative process" in the stammer and rubble of free association. I needed to find in the world what I feared was lacking in myself. Children are taught to stay put if they get lost in the woods. I circled around the search party in panicked circles. My poetry could not find me. You put a stop to all that.

"X marks the spot," you said, "X is your work."

So this weekend I will seal over unasked questions with a silence thick as sap, like an old tree healing a burn. Yet this man surprises me with his inquisitiveness and a gentleness that assumes nothing, and the little animal in my heart lifts its head to the wind and sniffs: *something for me, something for me.*

His eyes are pale with churned particles of stone, opaque and silvery, pure and blue as glacial tarns. Your wife with her strong heart is in a basement full of tools. Suddenly I feel serene and secure, joyous at the thought of the great abundance of inventions free of their owners and not subject to interpretation. And it seems right the way I left your neighborhood, the picture in my mind like this: a young woman going fast in a bright car passes an old man talking a parrot out of a tree. He doesn't notice her, and she only notices him for a moment, though not unkindly.